# PEACOCKS
# ON
# PAINT CREEK

An Emma Haines
Kayak Mystery

By

TRUDY
BRANDENBURG

Photos: Cover - Copperas Mountain along Paint Creek by Trudy Brandenburg.
Acknowledgement – John Brandenburg holding Trudy Brandenburg when she was four months old on Copperas Mountain Road along Paint Creek, taken by Bessie Brandenburg.

ISBN- 13:  978-1484018538
ISBN- 10:    1484018532

John Brandenburg holding four-month-old
Trudy Brandenburg
at the base of Copperas Mountain
with Paint Creek in the foreground.

*To my dad,*
*John Brandenburg,*
*the first person to show me*
*Paint Creek.*

# ACKNOWLEDGEMENTS

An "eddy-catching" thank you to my paddling friends, Tim Oyer, Empress Bethel, Larry Chaney, and John Victor who helped me calculate and visualize the opening scenes as we kayaked on Paint Creek, past the Copperas Mountains. "*How many yards away is that…*"

A kayak paddle salute to my editor and writing coach, Kelly Ferjutz. Also thanks to authors Deanna Adams and Claudia Taller for hosting writing conferences and retreats that help make this series possible. And thanks to author Les Roberts, for his feedback on my manuscripts and for always cheering me on.

And a deep thanks to my dad for showing me Paint Creek when I was four months old. Who would've known that forty-one years later I'd be paddling that creek dozens of times and writing about it? I love you and miss you every day.

Many thanks to my family and friends and my kayaking partners on the water.

And a special thanks to you, the fans and readers of *The Emma Haines Kayak Mystery Series.*

# CHAPTER 1

Friends, Emma Haines and Charles Wellington, had followed each other from Clintonville, Ohio, south on Route 104, hauling their kayaks on their vehicles. They had stopped at the First Capital Bed and Breakfast in Chillicothe, Ohio, and checked into their rooms.

From the B&B, they'd followed each other to the Blain Highway river bottom along Paint Creek where they would end their four hour kayak trip. The place where paddling trips end are referred to by people that kayak and canoe as the 'take-out.'

There were no other vehicles parked at the take-out as a great blue heron glided silently over them, flapping its slate-gray colored wings and giving them a bored glance.

The rising sun would soon warm the crisp October morning. Wisps of clouds dotted the blue sky, as if an artist had stroked it lightly with a brush. The air smelled of dew and the fading fall with a sliver of winter riding the breeze.

Charles and Emma lifted her blue Perception kayak, named *Arlene*, out of the bed of her white Tacoma pickup and onto the roof-rack of Charles's Lexus LX 570 SUV. It bumped his Dagger kayak and it nearly slid down the windshield onto the hood. Emma grabbed the nose of the boat and pushed it back.

"Do be careful, Emma. Don't you dare put a scratch on this vehicle."

"Why do you tell me that every time we load boats? Don't worry." She made quote signs with her fingers as she said, "I won't scratch your $82,000 baby. I'd have thrown my body across the hood and taken the hit." She clutched her heart.

He rolled his eyes. "I tell you because you need to be reminded every time. You're used to tossing boats into the lined bed of your truck without a second thought," he said as he secured the tie-downs over their kayaks.

"What's your point?"

"You know exactly what my point is."

"What, that I'm rough? I'm forgetful? Why don't you just buy a pickup to drive when you kayak? It's not like you can't afford one."

"You, of all people, should know that I would never be seen in a *pick-up truck*," he said as he climbed behind the steering wheel and shut the door.

She hit her remote to lock her truck and got in Charles's SUV. Her truck would stay parked at the take-out and they would ride in Charles's SUV upstream to where they would begin their trip, called the 'put-in.'

When they ended their trip at the take-out, they'd put their kayaks in the back of Emma's truck and drive back to the put-in where Charles's SUV would be parked. There, Charles would put his boat back on his SUV and follow Emma to the bed and breakfast. The use of vehicles to haul boats and people to and from a put-in and take-out is called 'shuttling.'

"They make fancy trucks for affluent snobs like you. Wouldn't hurt your image at all," she said, shutting her door and fastening the seatbelt.

He ignored her comment, as he often did, and drove up the steep gravel incline from the river bottom, turned left onto Blain Highway, and hung another left west onto Route 50.

Silence fell between them. Emma glanced at Charles then out the window, watching the fall colors scroll by. Fall was her favorite time of the year and she loved

2

kayaking down Paint Creek through the hillsides full of colored trees.

She scanned the two-lane road over the hood and remembered her father driving her and her mother on this road when she was a child to visit her mother's family and the road being covered by Paint Creek. Her father would creep through the flooded roadway, the tall tailfin brake lights shining red on the 1957 Chrysler as the water lapped at the hubcaps. Over the years, stream control had eliminated the flooding.

"You've been acting rather odd this morning, Emma. Something troubling you?"

They drove past the Dairy Bar and through Bournville, passing the Bell Tower banquet facility and the Valero gas station on their left.

"Have you heard from Simon?" she asked.

He took a slow deep breath. "You know I haven't heard from him since he walked out on me nearly three years ago. Why on earth do you ask?"

She stared out the windshield again as they passed Jones Levee Road. Her stomach did a small lurch as she turned toward him. "Simon called me last week."

"What?" He yelled, nearly jerking the vehicle off the road, turning his head toward her. "From Spain?"

"No. He's here. I mean, back home. In Clintonville."

"What? He's in Clintonville? He called you last week and you've said *nothing* to me about it? I can't believe you'd do this to me. The nerve of you. I simply cannot believe this."

"Calm down. Calm down. I think he was using me as a test run, but it didn't go so well for him. Maybe that's why he didn't call you. I ripped him to shreds before I hung up on him. He didn't have time to say anything except that he was in town and that he hadn't talked to you and wondered how you were doing. I told him if he was so concerned about you, he should call you, not me."

A heavy silence followed.

"How could you do this to me?" Charles finally said.

"I'm sorry. I thought maybe he might have called you and you just wanted to keep it to yourself. I really didn't want to hurt you and I wasn't sure what to do—or say. I'm sorry. This is between the two of you. My place is not in the middle of it. I have no idea why he called me."

Charles's face turned red and his knuckles grew white as he gripped the steering wheel. He glared out the windshield. His left pinky twitched spasmodically as they rode in silence for the next nine miles to the put-in.

Simon Johnson and Charles had lived together for twenty-three years before Simon walked out of their house one evening during dinner. Without any warning he announced that he was moving to Spain. That was nearly three years ago and Charles still couldn't think of it without feeling the pain all over again.

They'd been one of those couples that would never break up, or so everyone thought, including Charles. He never understood what had happened nor why Simon had walked out, no matter how much his engineer's brain analyzed it.

Charles glanced at Emma. He wanted to slap her.

They pulled into the clearing below Bainbridge, Ohio, the put-in where boaters and fishermen park their vehicles and launch their man-powered boats onto the creek. Years ago the spot was known as Twin Bridges because two wooden bridges stood beside each other, one for vehicles and horse and buggies and the other for the train. Even today, people still referred to the spot as Twin Bridges or Double Bridges or Two Bridges.

Charles started to get out of the vehicle.

"Charles," Emma said, leaning over and grabbing his arm. "Please don't be mad."

"I don't care to discuss it."

"Maybe we *should* talk about it."

"Let's just go kayaking." He got out of the vehicle and slammed the door.

"Damn it," she said, thumping her fists on the tops of her legs. She got out and helped Charles unload the kayaks and gear.

A red Jeep Liberty covered in mud from bumper to bumper was parked near the road at the pull-off. A beat-up blue pickup truck was parked about twenty feet from it.

"That guy's been doing some serious mud running," Emma said as she helped Charles lift his kayak from the roof rack and place it on the ground. He turned toward the Jeep.

"Appalling." He shuddered in disbelief. "That is absolutely not a way to respect a vehicle. I hope the driver is pulled over and ticketed."

"Believe it or not, the cops have more important things to do than deal with people who drive dirty cars. You're in the country now, City Boy. Probably belongs to a farmer who grows food for your favorite five star restaurants. Not everyone has their car waxed once a week at a detail shop like you."

"The roadways would look much better if everyone kept their vehicles clean. It would make this wonderful country even more beautiful."

"Why don't you write your Congressman? Sounds like an entire political campaign could be built around it; a new one. In fact it would be much easier for someone to enforce; easier than trying to deal with healthcare, the budget, foreign affairs, gun control, you know, that menial stuff. Some politician would probably jump all over it."

"I'd certainly consider giving them my vote," Charles said. "Maybe I am onto something, Miss Smartass. Now, help me carry my boat to the water."

"Just drag it in the grass."

"I do not *drag* my boat anywhere. That's one way I keep it looking new. Plus waxing it."

She sighed, picked up the stern of his kayak by the handle, and they carried it to the bank and set it down.

"Water looks good, it's up and moving. Surprising since it hasn't rained in over a week down here. Glad we caught the dam release," she said, holding her hand over the brim of her ball cap to look downstream. The water twinkled in the sunlight like cut glass.

Charles buckled his life jacket, put his boat in the stream, sat down, picked up his graphite paddle, and gracefully slid onto the creek like a swan. The sun reflected off the water in his RayBans which were propped on his chiseled nose above his salt and pepper mustache.

Emma walked back up the hill and dragged her boat through the grass to the bank, fastened her life jacket, got in her kayak, and pushed herself onto the stream.

The kayak had been a gift from Emma's good friend, Arlene, who had, unfortunately, lost her brave battle with myeloma cancer several years prior and Emma thought it only right to name the kayak after her.

Emma and Charles paddled easily, floating with the

current under the bridge going over Rt. 50. Bobbers hanging from the wires near the bridge were silent testimony of those fishermen who had bad luck on a cast. They paddled toward the first bend to the left where they would pass along the bottom of what was known as Little Copperas Mountain. Downstream, they would pass the main Copperas Mountain.

Both of the Copperas Mountains are ridges along the northeast creek bank, made of various types of shale. The larger of the two rises three-hundred fifty feet above Copperas Mountain Road, a dirt road running along its base. Gutters and channels running down the mountainsides make them look like a scene from out west. Tiny bits of shale often rolled down their faces. Trees hung over the top of their crests by their roots. A few scruffy trees' roots were wrapped around rocks. Emma and Charles never grew weary of the mountains' magnificent beauty.

The leaves were at their peak and the hills resembled an oil canvas, covered with splats of gold, green, brown, red, and yellow. Several Canada geese took off in front of them, honking as they ran along the water to get airborne. They paddled around several strainers – the word kayakers use to describe partially-submerged trees in the water.

"Fall is my favorite time of the year to paddle and it'll be one of the last good days before we have to get out the wetsuits. But we could have another Indian summer," Emma said.

"Perhaps," Charles replied.

Paint Creek is a tributary of the Scioto River. It meanders through five counties for ninety-five miles, with its headwaters beginning in Madison County before meeting the Scioto River near Chillicothe. The area was a popular hunting ground for the Shawnee.

In 1795, Nathanial Massie attacked a band of

camping Shawnee while surveying around Paint Creek. This ambush created havoc in the peace treaty negotiations. The leader of the Shawnee tribe that was attacked, Pucksekaw, set out for revenge, but Chief Blue Jacket convinced Pucksekaw to retreat so negotiations could continue. Later, Massie founded the lands at the confluence of Paint Creek and the Scioto River and Chillicothe.

While paddling on Paint Creek and the Scioto River, Emma would often think about the Shawnee Indians who had originally named the area, Chillicothe, meaning Principle Town. It was the first and third Capitals of Ohio during the 1800's.

In 1806, architect Benjamin Henry Latrobe, then working on the U.S. Capitol building, was asked by Thomas Worthington to build his family home in Chillicothe. Finished in 1811, the estate house, called Adena, was where Worthington and his wife, Eleanor, raised their ten children.

In 1918, at Chillicothe's Camp Sherman, 21,000 men stood in formation to create a picture of President Woodrow Wilson. It was also home to the summertime theatrical event, *Tecumseh,* which Emma and Charles loved to attend.

Chillicothe was also home to Archie Goodwin, the fictitious character in the Nero Wolfe detective series written by Rex Stout. Emma thought of her office manager and right hand man, Merek Polanski, as her Archie, except Merek was Polish, tattooed and pierced, and wore lots of leather rather than the styled hats, suits, ties, and wing-tip shoes so favored by the fictional Archie of the forties and fifties. And Merek hated milk. Archie Goodwin loved milk.

Emma had grown up in Chillicothe and she always enjoyed going back to its rolling hills, home to Mount Logan which is pictured in the Great Seal of the State of

Ohio as seen from the Adena Mansion. She also liked driving through its unique downtown architecture and remembering storefronts when she lived there. Only a few were the same. Her heart ached whenever she passed the burned out shell of the once beautiful Carlisle Building, built in 1885. She'd loved going to its shops and eating at The Harvester Restaurant and Cellar.

Sometimes when they'd come to town, she and Charles would paddle with the local kayak club, Southern Ohio Floaters Association, known as SOFA. And they always loved to eat at their favorite pizza place, Jerry's Pizza on Paint Street.

Soon after graduation from high school, Emma was hired by Matrix Insurance in Clintonville, Ohio. During the next twenty years, she worked her way up the ladder in the special investigative claims unit, also known as SIU, to the position of a well-respected insurance fraud investigator. She loved the job until the day an arsonist took a shot at her. Fortunately, she tripped just before the bullet flew over her head, but the experience had rattled her.

She decided to become a consultant and train investigators rather than be one. Five years ago, she'd established H.I.T., Haines Insurance Training, her consulting firm, and Matrix was her main client. But she still missed the thrill of cracking fraud cases in the field.

Emma had kayaked and rafted on dozens of streams all over the country, but Paint Creek was her favorite. She loved the scenery and the diversity of its different sections that she'd paddled over the years. She enjoyed the Paint's easy flow and navigation. The few strainers weren't difficult to paddle around and depending on the water level, the Paint could be a bouncy rapid-ride in the rocky spots when it was high, or offer the challenge to navigate like a pinball when it was low.

There were only a few houses along its shores, but the increasing amount of trash over the years was a growing concern among paddlers. She and Charles, and other paddlers she knew, collected it as they paddled. Paint Creek was a beautiful stream offering a unique enjoyment of nature for centuries and deserved respect and human stewardship.

Few song birds remained in the creek valley at this time of the year, having raised their young and flown off for warmer places. But many didn't migrate, including king fishers, hawks, cardinals, chickadees, owls, great blue herons, and the local eagles.

Charles looked at the sky. He blocked the sun with his left hand and pointed. "Is that an eagle?"

She looked up. "Good eye, Mr. Wellington." They watched the bird soar in lazy circles so high, they could barely make out the white head and white strip under its tail. A few times when it flew lower, the sun reflected off its yellow beak.

"Look, there's another one," she said, pointing.

"They're magnificent creatures. Breath taking," he said.

They floated in their kayaks and watched the birds, making an occasional stroke to keep their boats on course.

"This is why bird watchers have neck problems," she said, gazing up at the sky, rubbing the back of her neck. "Reminds me, I need to have Merek schedule a massage for me."

They paddled in silence for a few minutes.

"Did you really rip him to pieces?" Charles asked, not looking at her.

"I did."

He looked back at the sky. She paddled closer to him.

"Do you really want Simon back in your life after he walked out on you?"

He didn't answer. He took several strokes and paddled ahead of her.

A breeze ruffled her short brunette pony tail. She took a long stroke with the left blade of her paddle and watched the swirls it left behind in the water.

As they followed the sharp bend to the left that ran along the base of big Copperas Mountain, two men kayaked about twenty yards in front of them. The man to their left was in a red kayak, to their right, a green one. They occasionally turned to one another, talking.

Emma laid her paddle across the cockpit of her boat and watched the men. She wondered if one of them was the mud runner in the red Jeep.

She and Charles floated down the stream in silence, taking in the scenery and glancing up the slate mountainside to their right.

The stream gurgled over the rocks, a kingfisher twittered in the distance, and water dripped off their paddles and lapped at the sides of their kayaks. A turtle slid into the creek from the bank and a cardinal sang in the distance as a small white butterfly danced crazily down the stream in front of them.

# CHAPTER 2

"Bwwwaaaaaaaahhhhhhmmmmmmmm."

Birds burst from the woods, flying in all directions, as the sound from a gunshot, fired from the left bank, rumbled through the valley. Emma and Charles both jumped. She knew from her insurance training days, it was the sound of a high-powered rifle.

Slate from Copperas slid down the face of the hill, causing a small avalanche. Rocks the size of basketballs rolled and bounced and a few larger ones went off the dirt road and tumbled into the stream in front of them.

Ahead of them, the man in the red kayak slumped forward, dropping his paddle in the water. The other man paddled closer to him and grabbed his boat.

"He's hit. Get down! Lay down in your boat! Get down!" Emma screamed. She pawed her life jacket, grabbing for her whistle, as she slid down as far as she could into her boat. Charles did the same. She found her whistle and blew it hard, heart pounding, looking in the direction where the shot had come from. Charles blew his whistle too.

"Kayakers on the river! Hold your fire! Kayakers on the river!" they yelled.

A movement of blue and black between two trees shifted away from the river bank. Emma raised herself in her boat to get a better look. It was someone running from the creek through the woods. She sat up straight in her boat.

"Charles, go help that man. I'm going after that guy." She nodded toward the shore, paddling hard.

"Emma! Don't chase him. He has a gun, for God's

sake!"

"Just do it, Charles," she yelled, leaning forward, heading toward the left river bank. Charles shook his head, turned, and paddled fast to get to the men in front of them.

Seconds later she jumped out of her boat, yanked it up the bank with the bow handle, tossed her paddle into the cockpit, and started running through the woods after the person who had probably pulled the trigger.

Whoever was running from her was of a smaller build and had long, black hair that fell to the middle of his back. He was wearing a blue, hip-length jacket. The runner appeared to be in good shape, jumping over downed trees, and running through thickets, wild rosebushes, and poison ivy that had already turned red.

"Ouch," she yelled as a rosebush snagged her thigh through her splash pants. She unsnagged the bush and continued the chase.

"Stop or I'll shoot," she yelled a second before she tripped over a log and fell flat. She lay sprawled on the ground.

"Damn it!" she said, but it came out "Bbmmmmiiiihd," as she talked into a pile of dead leaves. All the shooter had to do now was come back and put a bullet in her back. But the person kept running in the other direction through the woods.

By the time she stood, spit the leaves and dirt out of her mouth and brushed herself off, there was no way she'd catch up with the person now. She made it to the edge of the woods that ran along the corn field.

The same muddy Jeep that had been parked at the put-in swerved up the dirt road running along the field, throwing dirt and dust behind it.

She trudged back through the woods, put *Arlene* in the water again, and paddled across the creek to the base of Copperas Mountain.

Charles paced on the dirt road, talking on his iPhone. The men's kayaks were lined up along the bank.

The man who had been shot sat leaning against a tree. A gauze bandage covered his forehead. He turned his head upward and said something to the other man standing beside him.

Charles walked to the edge of the water and pulled her boat onto the bank, still talking on his phone. He ended the call.

"The authorities are on their way. Emma, this is West Virginia all over again. I simply cannot believe this. I'm not sure I wish to continue boating with you if you're going to attract these unsuitable problems."

Four months ago, they'd met a convict on the New River in West Virginia named Earl "the Pearl" Calhoon who had tried to kill them. But Emma's quick thinking saved their lives and she stuck around, helped the authorities catch and put him away, and solved a forty-year-old mystery in the process.

"Yeah. Whatever, Charles. At least this time I don't think they were shooting at us. How is that guy?" she looked toward the man with the bandage on his head.

"He's extremely lucky. Shaken, obviously. The bullet skimmed his forehead, but didn't enter his skull. Rather amazing, actually. If he'd taken one more stroke or just tilted his head forward the slightest bit, he'd been shot through his left temple, no doubt about it; killed, most assuredly. The wounded man is Alder Mycon and the other is his brother, Forrest. I cleaned and dressed the wound. Did you see the shooter?"

She shook her head. "Just his back, his hair, and his getaway ride. He's the mud runner in the Jeep that was parked at the put-in. Hit the sheriff's number again. I need to report it right now. Your dream of the cops busting a dirty car driver may come true after all."

Charles slid his fingers across the face of the phone, tapped it a few times, and handed it to her. She held it to her right ear.

"This is Emma Haines. I'm with Charles Wellington who just called and reported a shooting on Paint Creek. Yes. Yes. That's right. I chased the shooter into the woods after a single shot was fired that wounded a kayaker named Alder Mycon. Yes. Yes." She nodded.

"The shooter remained about thirty feet in front of me while I was in pursuit, but I lost him. He had long black hair, hanging down about mid-back, wearing a blue hip-length jacket, black pants, maybe dark brown work boots, carrying what was probably a rifle. About five-five, I'm guessing, medium to small build, pretty good shape from the way he moved.

"He ran through the woods to the edge of the cornfield and fled in a red Jeep Liberty. It was parked at the clearing by the Paint Creek bridge when we pulled up. You can't miss it. It's covered in mud, from bumper to bumper, roof to wheels, totally covered in mud. You can barely make out the color, but you'd better hurry before the driver gets to a car wash."

Emma listened and nodded.

"Yes, that's correct."

She listened again and then spelled her name. "Yes, you can reach me at this number and I'll give you mine too, but I don't have my phone with me right now."

When the call ended, she handed the iPhone back to Charles and he tapped the screen and slid it into his nylon, water-proof pants pocket and zipped it.

"When are you going to buy an iPhone and stop using mine all the time?" Charles asked. "I'm not your data plan."

"You know I hate those things and I just don't like to carry my cell because I'm afraid it'll get wet. I kayak to get away from the phone, not take it with me. I'm not as important as you are. And besides, I have you and Merek," She gave him a curt smile and walked past him toward the men. He followed.

"Alder and Forrest Mycon, I'm Emma Haines, Charles's paddling partner. How are you, Mr. Mycon?" Emma asked Alder.

He looked up at her. He was young; late twenties, early thirties. He had intelligent dark brown eyes, and his sandy hair was clean and well-cut. His green flannel shirt and yellow t-shirt were mostly hidden under a gray Northface jacket. Khaki nylon pants, Keen sandals and waterproof socks completed his impressive and expensive outfit for kayaking.

"I'm—"

"Didja see who tried to kill my brother? I seen you go after her," Forrest interrupted as he stood beside them.

Emma looked the man over.

*These men are brothers?*

Forrest had long, brown greasy hair and wore a faded, torn blue flannel shirt, dirty blue jeans, and work boots. His eyes were brown and hollow. He had three missing teeth in the top left front of his mouth, surrounded by scraggly facial hair that hadn't seen a razor in days.

"Her? How do you know it was a woman?" she asked.

Forrest pushed rocks with the toe of his worn work boot, shoved both hands in his jeans pockets, and sucked in his breath. The air going through his teeth made an odd whistling noise. He breathed out. Everyone stared at him.

He shrugged. "Don't know. Just blurted it out. So,

did you see who it was? We got a right to know."

"Did *you* see who shot your brother?" she asked.

He shook his head. "We got a right to know who you saw though."

"Yes, you certainly do have a right to know, but it's best that we wait until the sheriff gets here to talk about it."

"My brother's just been shot. We got a right to know if you seen someone or not. Right now."

Emma gave Forrest a stern look before she squatted in front of Alder. Forrest leaned in closer. A funny aroma surrounded him.

"You need anything? Water? Anything?" Emma asked Alder.

"No, thank you. Your boyfriend, Charles, fixed me up nicely and gave me water. He must be a doctor. Damndest thing. I haven't been kayaking on this creek since I was a kid and this happens." He touched the bandage on his forehead and nodded toward Charles.

Emma smiled at Charles. "He is a doctor and knows a lot about chemistry and taking good care of people."

Charles gave her a small smile. He blushed, took off his ball cap, and ran his fingers through his thick graying hair.

"Some crazy person tried to shoot you, brother. I still can't believe it," Forrest piped up. He began pacing.

Alder turned toward Emma. "This is crazy. I mean, Forrest asked me to come and paddle with him and this happens. He said I'd been working on the farm too hard lately, and I needed a break, plus he needed to talk to me about something. I had to agree with him. I've been working from sunup to sundown, seven days a week for several weeks, harvesting my crops. I should be there now, but he convinced me to come."

"You have a vehicle at Jones Levee Road? That where you were taking out?" Emma asked.

Alder nodded. "Yeah. My truck's there."

"Water's running pretty fast. You must've planned for a quick trip," she said.

He shrugged. "I really never thought about it. Forrest told me to meet him at Jones, then we threw my boat into the back of his pickup and went to Twin Bridges."

"You see any other cars parked at Twin?"

Alder thought about it and nodded.

"Don't know what kind, but it was filthy. All covered in mud."

"What about you, Forrest? See any other vehicles at Twin Bridges when you put-in?"

Forrest nodded and looked at Alder. He dug a pack of Marlboros from his shirt pocket, shook one out, and lit it with a grimy red Bic lighter in a trembling hand. The smell of cigarette smoke floated through the valley. Charles scrunched his nose and walked away.

"It was a red Jeep Liberty's what it was."

"Probably just a hunter, or a drunk with bad aim. I mean, who would want to shoot me? It had to be an accident. I'm just a farmer." Alder's voice grew louder. "All I know is I was sitting in my boat and the next thing I know, I heard a shot. My forehead felt like it had been sliced by a hot knife. I smelled skin burning and I couldn't see when the blood ran into my eyes."

"I bet I know who'd want to shoot you." Forrest said, blowing smoke out of his bony nose. All eyes turned toward him. In the distance, the sounds of sirens and vehicles bouncing over the dirt road grew louder.

"How 'bout that ex-wife of yours? I bet she'd love to shoot you. Damn woman," Forrest snarled as he blew out another stream of smoke.

"That's the dumbest thing I've ever heard. Why would Tammy want to shoot me?" Alder snapped. "Just because you hate her doesn't mean she's responsible for every bad thing that happens in my life."

"Well, I wouldn't put nothin' past that one, I wouldn't," Forrest said. He took another long drag of his cigarette. "And I know she drives a red Jeep, just like that one sittin' at the put-in, all covered in mud."

"The authorities have arrived," Charles said, rejoining them.

Copperas Mountain Road ran along the bottom of the mountain above the creek bank. Four cruisers, a sheriff's pickup truck with a row boat in the bed, and an ambulance stopped above them on the road. Even as the sirens quieted, their lights continued flashing red and blue on the hillside and the woods. Officers climbed out of the vehicles like ants, running toward them.

"Well, well. Here they come to save the ever-lovin' day," Forrest sneered as he flipped his cigarette butt into the creek. It sizzled and floated on the current.

Charles hurriedly walked downstream and scooped it up with a piece of bandage he had in his pocket and dropped it into a baggie.

"Disgusting," he whispered under his breath, zipping the baggie shut, and holding it away from him like a dirty diaper.

A tall thin blonde in uniform stepped in front of Emma and extended her hand. "Hello, I'm Detective Day with the Paintville Sherriff's Department," she said.

Emma shook her hand. Day was at least 6' 2", in her mid-thirties, and apparently worked out extensively, based on her neck muscles, hand shake, and protruding veins on the tops of her hand. Her long, blonde hair was pulled back in a ponytail, and her makeup was perfect, with a natural gloss on her lips—feminine while authoritative. Emma could picture her shooting hoops for a college team in the woman's past. She wore a huge set of wedding gear on her left hand.

"Emma Haines. Pleased to meet you."

The other officers were talking with Alder and Forrest while the medics tended to Alder's wound. Charles stood off to the side, talking on his iPhone again. He looked striking in his red jacket and black spray-pants, but then he always looked like he modeled for GQ magazine.

"Likewise. I understand you're the paddler who was with Charles Wellington and you both witnessed the shooting from behind the victim. And you chased a person you thought was the shooter through the woods on the opposite bank? We have two patrol cars searching for the Jeep you reported. We appreciate that."

"Forrest just told us that it is a Jeep like Alder's ex-wife drives."

Day lifted an eyebrow and stepped away. She talked into the microphone clipped on her shoulder, then walked back over to Emma.

Day smiled and looked Emma in the eye. "Thank you. Now, I need you to start at the beginning and tell me everything," she said, flipping a page in a small notebook she'd pulled from her pocket, pen at the ready.

"Of course. I understand. I'm a twenty-year insurance fraud investigator and now I train investigators. I've worked with lots of good cops over the years, all over the country."

"So you have a sense for this." Day said.

"Yes." Emma nodded. "I'll start at the beginning. Charles and I pulled into the turnoff at the bridge and unloaded our kayaks at about a quarter after ten. I always check my watch to time the trips," Emma told the story, and confirmed the contact information for her and Charles.

Five minutes later Day said, "Very thorough observations, Ms. Haines. I appreciate your help. Is there anything else you can think of that might help us?"

Voices chattered through the small radio clipped to Day's shoulder, but Emma couldn't make out what was being said.

"From investigator to investigator, may I be frank?"

"Of course. Please do."

"I'd lean on Forrest Mycon like rolling a boulder up that hillside." Emma pointed toward Copperas Mountain, behind them. "He doesn't seem too upset by this whole thing, and, like I said, he referred to the shooter as a "her." 'I seen you go after *her*.' I thought that was interesting. He said it very matter-of-factly and when I questioned him about it, he blew it off. Wouldn't answer me. And from where he was on the creek, I doubt he could've seen much of anything. He was on the other side of Alder and too far away. He mentioned that Alder's ex drives a Jeep like the one at the put-in.

"And those two brothers," Emma nodded toward them, "there's just something not right there. First off, they're as opposite as humans can be—looks, grammar, dress—you name it. They don't look like they'd be close pals, out for a friendly paddle. And Alder said that Forrest insisted they go on a kayak trip here, today, together, so they could talk. During harvest time, the second busiest time of year for a farmer. Water's up too, moving pretty fast. If they wanted a decent paddle, they'd probably take out at Blain, not Jones Levee. Or not be on here at all, if they haven't paddled in a while. Could be tricky at this level. It all just feels funny to me."

Day nodded and made more notes, closed the notebook and slid it back in her pocket. "Well, thank you, again, Ms. Haines. Could you and Charles please come to the patrol office and file an official report?"

"Of course. But Charles's SUV is back at the put-in below Bainbridge and mine's at Blain."

"Not a problem. We can load your boats in the back of the pick-up and take you to wherever you want to go." She pointed to the pickup.

Alder Mycon was being loaded into the back of the ambulance. Forrest stood beside the door. One of the medics asked him not to light a cigarette. Emma let out a long breath and shook her head. *What a piece of work.*

A Paint5 News van threw dust as it stopped to a sliding halt behind the cruisers.

"Thank you, again, Ms. Haines."

Day and Emma shook hands.

"Now if you'll excuse me. The press is here and I need to brief them." Davis walked quickly and confidently toward the van.

Charles strolled over to Emma. "I believe Mr. Forrest Mycon doesn't possess the intelligence of a blow fly," he said.

"You are Sherlock reincarnated, Mr. Wellington. Come on, we need to go to the cop shop."

"Of course, we do. What a surprise. Kayaking with you seems to take us there lately. Amazing."

"Never a dull moment with me, right?" Emma said, pointing to herself with both thumbs, raising her eyebrows, tilting her head, and giving Charles a cheesy smile.

Charles walked away toward the kayaks, shaking his head.

# CHAPTER 3

Charles and Emma got out of the police pickup at Blain. They loaded their kayaks into the back of Emma's pickup, and followed the patrol truck toward the sheriff's office.

"Any observations other than what we've discussed?" Emma asked Charles.

He shook his head. "None I can think of."

They rode in silence for several minutes before Charles said, "Mary called."

"When does she get back from New Zealand?"

"I'm to pick her up at the airport again tomorrow around five. It can be exhausting being the only child of the continuous champion of the Women's Silver Spikes World Golf Championship." He smiled and looked out the passenger window.

"So she won this tour too." Emma said, smiling. "That's awesome."

He nodded. "Yes. By several strokes. She's a natural. Sadly, golfing wasn't passed on in my DNA. I believe I might've enjoyed it more if I played a better game."

"Never played golf in my life and never intend to. I don't have the desire or the time."

"I'm surprised you don't get Merek to play for you. He does everything else for you."

"You're just jealous that you don't have a Merek. Maybe you should hire a personal assistant. You could certainly afford it. He—or she—could buy a pickup that would suit you."

Merek Polanski was Emma's right arm and managed both her personal and business schedules. She'd met him just days after she'd started her consulting firm, five years ago.

She'd walked into the local computer store and Merek had sold her a laptop. She was so impressed with him, she offered him a job right there as her assistant. He accepted and walked out the door with her, never looking back. Since that day, he'd run all her business and personal affairs and she paid him highly for it.

He'd lived in Poland most of his twenty-six years. He spoke English well, through a thick, Polish accent. He was a shrewd businessman and researcher and helped her with everything from writing all her presentations for Matrix to keeping track of her business and personal schedules. Sometimes, he'd even cook her Polish food, including her favorite, cheese and potato pirogies.

He was young, handsome, and covered with tattoos and piercings. He wore lots of leather and owned a Harley Davidson motorcycle as big as a Fiat. He was a huge part of Emma's business success and he gave her the freedom to go kayaking just about any time she wanted. They made a good team, Merek running the business and Emma presenting and training insurance investigators and—kayaking.

As Charles often did, he ignored her comment. "Who do you think you saw running through the woods?"

"Actually, it *could've* been a woman, I guess. Forrest said 'her.' Like he was sure it was a woman. A man would've been more likely to wear camo than a woman. The person had long dark hair and a blue lightweight jacket, not typical hunting clothes, but I don't think there's a hunting season going on now, anyway. I'm not ruling it out. But whoever it was drove that new, muddy red Jeep Liberty we saw at the put-in. Muddy. Why was it so muddy? It has to have been muddy for a long time, because there's been no rain around here in over three weeks. Everything's dry as a bone."

They continued to talk about what had happened until Emma pulled the truck into a visitor's space at the Paintville Sheriff's lot. They got out and went into the building and were escorted into a large room with a table and chairs. Day and a deputy entered and closed the door.

After statements were taken, they got back in Emma's truck and drove to Charles's SUV that was parked at Twin Bridges. From there, he followed her back to the B&B.

Emma parked her truck and walked over to Charles's SUV. He lowered his window.

"It's dinner time. I say we put our boats and gear in the garage, run in, clean up and change, and head to Jerry's to get a pizza. I'll drive. I promised Merek I'd bring him back a couple. I'll have to remember to pick them up before I head back home."

"I'm exhausted, but I can't pass up a Jerry's pizza," he said.

They put their boats and gear in the garage, locked the door, and went into the B&B to their rooms, showered, and met down in the foyer. As they walked through the small parking lot to Emma's truck, Charles sarcastically said, "You're not leaving tomorrow, are you, Sherlock?"

"Of course not."

"Yes. Shocking. Well, I'm leaving in the morning. I have errands to run before I pick up mother at the airport."

"I know. And even if you didn't have to pick up Mary, you'd leave anyway. This isn't your gig."

"You are absolutely correct. I leave the authorities in charge to catch criminals. You should do the same. You could've gotten killed in West Virginia and this could be a dangerous situation as well. You don't like getting shot at, remember?"

"Right. Get in."

It was seven on a Saturday night and Jerry's Pizza on Paint Street in Chillicothe was packed. And why wouldn't it be? Everyone loved the pizza and it was a popular weekend spot.

The lights were low and it was noisy as people yelled and laughed over ZZ Top's "Sharp Dressed Man" coming through the ceiling speakers.

A loud voice boomed from the bar, "And now she's trying to kill him. She tried to shoot him on the river today. I always told Alder that Tammy was no good for him at all. No good."

Forrest sat perched on a stool, his back leaning on the bar, drinking from a longneck Budweiser and holding court with several men sitting and standing around him.

"Quick, go toward the back. I don't want him to see us," Emma yelled into Charles ear.

Charles nodded.

They slid into a booth that had just been cleared which was a perfect spot for them to watch Forrest while still being hidden by the crowd. Often they could hear him yell and hoot.

"That bullet whizzed right by me after it caught Alder across the forehead. I could'ah been killed too, I tell ya. It- woulda gone thru his skull and then right through mine if we'd been an inch more downstream." His arms flailed as he told a colorful version of the day's events. He had on the same clothes he'd worn on the river.

A waitress took Emma's and Charles's orders, left and returned with their drinks. About ten minutes later, a steaming pizza was placed in front of them.

"What a character," Charles said as they watched Forrest weave his tale while eating their pizza. Charles snatched up the last corner piece and popped it into his mouth.

"Stay here," Emma said. He looked puzzled. She tossed her napkin onto the empty pizza pan, put her Fossil purse on her shoulder, slid out of the booth, and walked toward Forrest.

Charles watched, smiled, shook his head and leaned back against the seat. Four women eyed him as they walked by.

"Check that guy out. Never saw him before. Man, what a hunk," one of them yelled to the others.

He did look out of place, dressed like a New York model in a bar room full of people in comfortable flannel shirts and blue jeans with a few people in business clothes sprinkled in. But he didn't care. Charles was never out of place, it was the rest of the world that was. He always wore designer clothes and expensive accessories and looked distinguished, no matter his surroundings.

Forrest squinted as Emma parted the half circle of men who all held beers and checked her out.

One whistled. "Well, well. What do we got here?" the man to her right said.

Emma smiled. "Hey, Forrest. You doing okay? I was worried about you after what happened today."

Forrest squinted an eye at her and frowned. "Ahhh, you're that woman that was behind us on the water with her boyfriend."

"You never told us that part," one of the men said.

Forrest gave him a dirty look.

"Yeah, well, I was gettin' there. This here woman, what's your name again?"

"Emma."

"Yeah. Her and her boyfriend were behind us on the water and her boyfriend patched up Alder. Reckon it was mighty nice of him to do that."

A man handed him another beer. Forrest tipped it toward her in a salute before he took a long chug.

"You're welcome. Hey, you need a ride home? I'd like to talk to you about what happened today. I'd be glad to give you a lift."

"Whooohaaa, Forrest. Du-u-u-u-de. I think she's hittin' on you, man" one of the men said, elbowing another guy in the ribs and laughing.

All the men laughed and made a few more remarks before they began to disperse. After a few seconds, Emma stood alone in front of Forrest.

He pointed a finger at her. "Now, you listen to me, pretty little lady. You may want to go to bed with me and I'm all for it, just not tonight. I got business to attend to and I'll have to take a rain check."

He turned and plopped the bottle on the bar so hard that beer splashed out the top. He pushed himself from the bar, stood, and left through the front door.

Emma shook her head in disbelief, before she walked back over to Charles and sat in the booth.

"I'd say, you're losing your touch, Miss Charming. You ran him off rather quickly," Charles said with a smirk.

"Save it. Come on. We'll follow him."

"I thought we were going back to the bed and breakfast. I'm drained. I just want to retire for the evening."

"Stop whining. Come on. Hurry up."

"But—"

"Let's go."

They left Jerry's, walked across Paint Street, and climbed into Emma's truck. Forrest pulled out of the lot several spaces away in the blue, rusted pickup that had been parked at Twin Bridges.

"I look forward to this chase with ferocious suspense." Charles rolled his head toward Emma and took a deep breath. "Simon didn't say anything more, did he?"

"I thought you didn't want to discuss it."

"You're right. I don't."

She didn't reply. Several minutes passed.

"I'm so looking forward to returning home after I pick up Mary at the airport. I miss Ron and the boys."

Charles had three chocolate Labrador retrievers that he and Simon had adopted from the Labrador rescue; Sam, Cecil and Cleo, referred to as 'the boys.'

Emma glanced at him. His face reflected the light from a streetlamp. Meeting him sixteen years ago while riding their bikes in opposite directions while on their way to work on the Olentangy Bike Path in Clintonville had turned into a unique friendship. They'd stopped, chatted, and discovered they'd both liked the outdoors. Emma had taken him on his first kayaking trip and he'd been hooked ever since.

Charles was the chief engineer at Bridge Systems in Clintonville. He was in charge of a staff of two hundred plus people, working on confidential projects for NASA and the military. She'd learned not to ask him what he was working on because he could never tell her.

He'd been dating a former engineer at Bridge, for the second time around, Ron Tran, for nearly three months, but she knew he still missed Simon. *Sometimes you can't get through the strainers in life; you just have to paddle around them,* she thought.

Ron had been in a terrible car accident while leaving

Charles's house four months ago and Charles helped nurse him back to health, barely leaving his side. Ron told Charles he'd gotten a better offer at the structural science plant in Columbus, but deep-down, Charles felt that Ron had left Bridge so he could pursue Charles on Charles's terms—it was mandatory to keep work and dating entirely separate. They'd been seriously dating since Ron's departure.

At the time of Ron's accident, Emma was in West Virginia, tracking down Earl Calhoon. While she was there working the case, she'd met the handsome widower and local newspaper owner, Stratton Reeves, who'd helped her trap Calhoon and the crooked Chief of Police. He'd written the story about it for the *Stonefalls Post*, the local newspaper that he owned, and won another writing award to add to his collection.

He'd been a reporter and editor for *The New York Times* before he and his wife built their dream home on a mountain near Stonefalls, West Virginia. Of course, plans frequently go awry, and his wife, Ann, died after a long battle with cancer. Not knowing what to do with himself, Stratton had bought the newspaper.

Emma had no intention of falling in love. There's a reason they call it 'fall.' In her experience, romantic relationships were a waste of energy and time and in the end, only led to a broken heart and pain from the 'fall'. She'd had her heart broken once and decided that was enough. She also saw what happened to Charles and others around her. She knew Charles was trying to leave Simon behind and move on, but he'd 'fallen in love.' And what was scaring her now was, she enjoyed being with Stratton—a lot.

They drove out of town and through back country roads. "Where is this guy going?" Emma said, flipping her blinker to make a right turn.

Charles sat up as she drove past a small dark parking

lot, turned around in a drive, and parked along the side of the road away from the lot. He and Emma watched Forrest get out of his truck and go through a blue door into a ratty building. Several cars and pickups sat scattered in the lot. "What is this place?" he asked, frowning.

"The Blue Caboose," she said, reading a faded sign hanging above the door. "This place has been here forever, but I've never been inside."

An old brown Saturn coupe pulled into the lot. A man got out and walked quickly into the bar.

"I suppose that you are going to go in there *now*?" Charles asked.

"Not right now. I don't want him to know we're following him. I'll wait until he comes back out."

"*We* are not following him. *You* are. Emma, this could take all night." Charles crossed his arms in front of his chest, slid down in the seat, and closed his eyes.

Minutes later, Forrest came out, got in his truck and drove away.

"Fast drinker. I'll go in and ask around about ole' Forrest, see what I can find out. You stay here, and stay out of sight. I don't want anyone to see you. And call my cell in exactly ten minutes to get me out of there," she said.

Charles didn't open his eyes. "If I think of it. I'm tired. Let's go back to the bed and breakfast."

"You'd better think of it." She pulled her hair out of her pony tail holder, tossed the holder into the dash console, got out of her truck, and strutted into the bar.

It took several seconds for her eyes to adjust to the

dark in the small, old bar. The smell of cigarette smoke and fried food hung in the air. Even though smoking hadn't been permitted in Ohio bars for years, it certainly didn't mean everyone followed the rules. On the other hand, it could've been accumulating over decades and it was baked into every surface. No matter. It made her stomach queasy.

An old juke box sat in a corner under a blinking Coors sign. She hadn't seen a juke box like it since she was in junior high school. She walked to the bar and flashed her best smile at the bartender.

"Hey, there. I'd like a Bud in a bottle, please."

The young bartender had wild, blonde curly hair. He looked her over, no emotion on his bearded face. He reached a tattooed arm into a cooler, pulled out the beer, popped the cap, and set the beer in front of her without losing eye contact.

"Thanks." She turned and looked around the bar. The driver of the brown Saturn sat in a booth to her left. A few other people were scattered around the bar, a couple in the back, and two men sat at the end of the bar. Others sat at various tables on metal chairs. She turned back to the bartender and smiled.

"You know some guy named Forrest Mycon? I'm supposed to meet him here."

The bartender stared at her with a grimace, but said nothing.

"He's an old high school friend and I happened to be in town. We were supposed to meet here."

The bartender turned away from her for several seconds, picked up a bar rag, turned back around, and started wiping the bar. He finally looked up at her.

"Don't know him."

"Well, I was running late. He must've just got tired of waiting. Anyone come in and wait awhile then leave?"

"That'll be two bucks."

Emma opened her purse, dug out a ten, and tossed it on the bar. "Keep the change. And there's more where that came from if you know anything about him."

The bartender picked up the money and leaned toward her. "Come to think of it, some guy did come in here a little while ago, hung around awhile. He talked to that guy right over there." He nodded his head toward the Saturn owner.

She dug in her purse and laid another ten on the bar. "Thanks."

She turned and walked toward the booth where a small man sat with a half-full bottle of Miller in front of him. He wore a flannel shirt, dark pants, and work boots. The end of a stuffed white envelope stuck out of the top of his shirt pocket. He was peeling the label off the bottle, balling it up, and dropping the pieces on a napkin.

Emma stuck out her chest and cocked her right hip. She was a petite 5'4", 125 lbs., worked out, rode her bicycle, hiked, and kayaked. She was solid, in shape, and also well blessed in the bosom department. She gave her head a little toss, causing her brunette hair to fluff and lie on her shoulders.

"Hey, there," she said. "I'm from out of town. Where do people party around here?"

The man checked her out and smiled. "Well, pretty thing, if you just want to take a seat, I'll be glad to tell you."

"Thanks." She slid into the booth across from him. "My name's Emma. What's yours?"

"Jebediah Pierce is my name. My friends call me Jeb. Where you from, Emma?" He took a long pull on his beer.

"Nice to meet you, Jeb. I'm from up north. Came down here to meet an old high school friend. Bartender told me I just missed him and you might know him."

Jeb took another long drink of his beer and carefully put the bottle on the table. "And who might that be?"

"Forrest Mycon."

Jeb cocked his head to the side. "Nope. Sorry, don't know him."

"But the bartender said Forrest was talking with you a few minutes ago," she said with a girly tease mixed in with a whine.

He shook his head. "I haven't talked to anyone all night except you and him to get this beer." He looked over at the bartender and back at her.

Emma grinned. *Even. Lie for a lie.*

She leaned over the table and his eyes went exactly where she wanted them to go.

"You sure you don't know Forrest?" she said, smiling.

"I already told you, can't say that I do." He drank his beer keeping his focus on her cleavage.

"Well, it doesn't really matter, I guess. What do you do for a living?" She leaned back in the booth, still smiling at him.

He stared at his beer bottle then lifted it. "I'm a factory worker, a union man and proud of it."

"Right on," she said. She tipped her bottle toward him before she took a sip of beer. "Do you like to dance?"

"Not really."

"You've never danced with me, right?"

"Don't think so."

"You'll love it. Let me go see what's on that music box over there."

The man nodded and drank his beer as he watched her sashay toward the juke box in her t-shirt, shorts, and sandals. She wanted to give the man a little space and time to think. Maybe he'd change his mind and tell her about his conversation with Forrest.

She leaned over the list of songs, cocking her hip. She slid three quarters into the slot and chose Bob Seger's *Nightmoves*, rolled her eyes, walked back to the booth, and sat down.

"You know, we don't have to dance. We can just talk if you'd like."

The man nodded. "Fine by me."

"You from around here?"

The man nodded. "All my life."

"You're quite handsome." She took a quick drink of her beer. He wasn't a bad looking guy, but she certainly wouldn't call him handsome. She figured him to be in his late fifties–around Charles's age.

He nodded and took another swig of beer. Her cell rang and she pulled it out of her purse.

"Emma, what on earth are you doing in there? Get out here this instant."

"Oh, hi, Charlene," Emma said into her phone.

There was a pause before Charles sarcastically said, "I see. I assume you're talking with someone about him and you're '*undercover*'?"

"Yes. Yes. That's right. Okay. I'll meet you there in about twenty minutes."

"Five more minutes. Hurry up and get out here or I'm coming in and making a scene." He ended the call.

"Okay. Yes. I do want to see that movie. Yes. I'll be there."

Emma hit the end call key, slid her cell in her purse, and pretended to take a long swig of beer.

"Sorry 'bout that. It's my cousin, Charlene. She wants me to meet her at the movies. I guess I'd best be going."

"So, you got kin here?"

"Yeah. I lived here for a while, then got a job up north and moved away."

He eyed her. She could nearly hear the gears turning in his head.

"Your cousin as pretty as you?"

Emma giggled and shrugged. "You single, Jeb?"

The man nodded. "You?"

"I sure am. Maybe we could go to a movie sometime. You want my number?"

He shrugged. "Sure."

She dug in her purse for her pen and notebook and jotted her first name and cell on a piece of paper, ripped it out, and handed it to him.

He gave it a glance, folded it, and slipped it into his shirt pocket in front of the white envelope.

"I'll give you a call sometime."

"I hope you call me this week while I'm in town. I'm on vacation and need to get back home in a few days."

He shrugged and peeled more of the label off his beer bottle with a dirty thumb nail. "Sure, I can call this week."

"Good. I think we could have a real good time." She winked at him.

She slid out of the booth and walked out the door, swinging her small hips as much as she could.

She strutted through the parking lot, swaying her hips, and got in her truck. Charles was scrunched down in the passenger seat, pouting.

"Good grief. I nearly threw my back out. Stay down until we get out of here," she said.

He gave her a look. "Well, you should have. You looked ridiculous. Do men really go for that?"

She rolled her eyes. "What do you think?"

He shrugged and wrinkled his face like he'd tasted something bad. "I suppose you made new *boyfriends* then?" he asked.

"I sure did and I hope he calls me because I'd bet

he's lying about knowing Forrest and I'm going to find out why."

"Of course, you will."

She stuck her tongue out at him, started the truck, and drove to the First Capital Bed and Breakfast.

# CHAPTER 4

"As always, an exquisite breakfast, Robert," Charles said, patting his lips and mustache with a starched green napkin.

"Thank you, Charles. It's always a pleasure having you and Emma stay here. Clara and I enjoy cooking. It's one of the reasons we bought this place."

Robert and Clara Shaw owned the First Capital Bed and Breakfast of Chillicothe, Ohio. They had worked hard, both retirees from the local Glatfelter paper mill, still known as "the Mead," which had been the bread and butter for the city over the past 150 years. Before retiring, they'd purchased the beautiful Southern-styled mansion with plans for restoring it into a B&B.

They lived in the large suite on the third floor. The second floor was lined by six bedrooms, each with its own fireplace and bathroom. The first floor held the kitchen, dining area and a large sitting room and small public office for guests to use. Charles and Emma had stayed there many times over the years and they'd all become friends.

Charles folded his napkin and placed it on the table. He picked up his coffee.

"A terrible thing, the shooting on the river yesterday. I read about it in this morning's paper," Robert said. "At least no one was seriously injured. It sounds as if it could've been fatal and you two could've been killed too. My word!"

"Yes, we were all extremely lucky," Charles said, giving Emma a look.

"Robert, do you know the Mycon brothers?" Emma

asked, looking away from Charles and spearing a sausage from her plate.

"I really don't know them, but I'm well aware of who they are. Everyone in the county is aware of the Mycon family."

"What can you tell me about them?"

"I can tell you that one is as nice and decent a man as can be and the other is simply trash, along with the sister, Willow. Hard to believe they all three had the same parents."

"Willow?"

"Yes, Willow. I heard his father loved trees, thus, Forrest. Willow. Alder. You get the picture."

"So, one veneer quality and two rotten trees?" Emma asked between bites.

Robert chuckled. "Very rotten. Forrest has been in and out of the local jail so many times, I wouldn't be surprised if they keep a cell open just for him. And the sister, she's another story altogether. She has five children, all with different fathers. She lives in a trailer somewhere outside of town. From the looks of her, I'm not sure how she could entice any man, but they say there's someone for everyone," Robert gracefully moved around the table. "Are you finished, Charles?"

He nodded. "Yes, again. Thank you. It was delicious. I'd like the recipe for that egg casserole. There's a spice in there, I just can't quite distinguish."

Robert smiled and nodded as he picked up Charles's plate. "I'll write it down for you before you leave." He walked out of the dining room into the back kitchen.

Charles checked his Rolex. "Emma, I'm leaving as soon as I'm finished packing. Why don't you follow me back?"

Emma peered at him over her coffee cup.

"Ahhhh, yes. Just as I suspected. You're really not coming back. You're going to stay here and find the perpetrator who shot Alder Mycon."

"Yes. I'm going to stay and find out who fired that shot. It could've just as easily hit one of us, you know."

"Yes, but it didn't." Charles pushed himself away from the table. "You'll do what you need to do, I know. Just be careful. I'll call you later."

"Are you still upset about Simon calling me?"

He sighed, bent down, and kissed the top of her head.

"Be careful," he repeated before he left the dining room.

Two hours later, Emma pulled into the hospital parking lot. She got out of her truck, locked the doors with her remote, and stopped at the information desk. After locating the elevator, she rode up to the fourth floor and found room 412. Knocking lightly on the door she waited for a response.

"Come on in," Alder's voice came from the other side.

She opened the door and stuck her head in. "Hi, Alder. Remember me?"

"Yes, of course. Emma,right?"

"That's right. Is it okay if I come in?"

"Sure, sure. Come on in and have a seat."

Alder sat up in bed and smiled at her. He was a handsome man, even with a bandage across his forehead; thick chest, bulging arm muscles, and an intelligent, young face.

"How're you doing?" she asked.

"Good. They say I can probably get out of here tomorrow. I guess they still want to keep me around for observation, even though I feel fine. Sheriff Day just left."

"Nice lady. Do you know her?" Emma asked.

"She does seem nice and is really concerned. But, no, I've never met her before. I've never had much experience with the law. In fact, this could be my first time."

"Well, that's good, right?"

"I suppose so," he said.

"I'd like to talk to you about what happened yesterday. Is that okay?"

"Sure. I mean, you and your boyfriend really helped me and I appreciate it."

"No problem." She pulled a chair from the wall and sat down beside the bed. "Alder, do you have any idea who might've fired that shot?"

He pursed his lips and shook his head. "Like I just told the sheriff, I don't have a clue. Not a single one. Day asked me if I had any enemies, all that kind of stuff. But, really, not that I know of. I still think it was an accident. Someone out with a gun, hunting."

"Not sure what they'd be hunting or why they'd be shooting in that direction."

Alder thought about that and shrugged. "Beats me. I really have no idea what happened. All I know is I'm a lucky man." He touched the bandage on his head.

"I have to agree with that."

The door to the hospital room opened. Forrest charged into the room along with a large woman dressed in a worn, flowered-print, polyester pantsuit who waddled in after him. Emma was glad Charles wasn't there to see her; he would've had a fashion-induced coronary. Every roll was wrapped tight and bounced as she moved. She had long stringy brown hair and resembled Forrest.

"What are *you* doing here, lady?" Forrest asked,

giving Emma a surprised look.

She didn't answer.

"Who are you?" asked the woman.

"She's that woman I told you about. Her and her boyfriend were the ones behind us on the river yesterday," Forrest said.

The woman gave Emma a disapproving look. "Oh."

"And who might you be?" Emma asked, already knowing it was Willow.

The woman looked Emma over. "I'm Willow. These here are my brothers."

"Pleased to meet you, Willow."

"They find out who shot my brother?" Forrest asked her.

"Not that I know of. Do you have any ideas who might have wanted to shoot your brother?"

"I sure do. I already told you, it was that damn ex-wife of his, Tammy. Her car was there. It was her."

"It wasn't Tammy. I keep telling *you that*," Alder said, his voice rising.

"I'd bet it was her too." Willow said. "She never got over your divorce. You know how she is, Alder."

"Yes, I do. And that's why I know she wouldn't shoot me."

"What'd you see when you run after the person?" Forrest asked Emma.

She said nothing.

"The sheriff told me you saw a person with a blue jacket on and long black hair running through the woods," Forrest said.

"Sherriff Day told you that?" Emma asked.

"That's right." Forrest nodded his head once and stuck out his bottom lip.

"Well, there you have it," Willow said, wedging herself on the ledge of the window. "Tammy has long black hair and a blue jacket. I saw her wearin' it in the

42

grocery just the other day." The three of them looked at Emma. She turned to Alder.

"Is that true?"

Alder shrugged and looked away. "She might have a blue jacket. I don't really know."

"It was her, I'm tellin' you. You should tell the sheriff to go pick her up."

Alder stared down at his hands crossed in his lap. "Tammy would never shoot me."

"But she was always mad that you cheated on her, Alder. She's a vengeful woman," Willow said.

"That's right, bro," Forrest agreed.

Alder sighed. "I don't care to talk about this right now." He glanced at Emma with an embarrassed look on his face.

"Why you stayin' around here? I figured you and your boyfriend left." Forrest sneered at Emma.

"Well, as you can see, no, I haven't left."

"When you leavin'?"

"I haven't decided."

"Why you stayin' around here for?" Willow asked.

Emma shrugged. "Just curious. I'd like to know who shot your brother. They could've just as easily been shooting at me and my friend. Or shooting at you and missed and hit your brother," Emma said, glaring at Forrest. The room went silent.

"Well, I got to be goin'," Willow slid off the windowsill like a giant glob of melting plastic that had been poured into tubing. "You call me if you need anything, okay?" she said to Alder.

"Me, too. I gotta go, too," Forrest chimed in.

"Hey, Forrest. Got a quick question for you," Emma said.

Forrest and Willow both stopped and turned to look at her.

"You had a couple of pretty nice looking boats out

there." She looked at Forrest then at Alder. "Just wondered where you got them."

"Forrest had the boats and paddles and things."

Everyone looked at Forrest.

Forrest's smile was wicked. "Borrowed 'em off a friend. He loaned them to me. I got lots of friends," he said.

"I'll bet you do. You're just a friendly kind of guy," Emma said holding his gaze.

Forrest gave her a dirty look and sniffed loudly. Tension hung in the air. Emma turned, walked to the other side of the room, and looked out the window.

"Well, thanks for stopping by. I'm feeling much better," Alder said.

After grumbling something indecipherable, Forrest and Willow stalked out of the room.

Alder glanced at Emma and back out the window. "Quite a crew, I'd guess is what you're thinking."

"Honestly, yes," she said. "Are they your step-siblings or were you adopted? Are you close?"

He shook his head. "No. We're blood-related, and no, we're not close. Not at all."

"But you were kayaking with your brother yesterday."

Alder nodded. "Like I told you, he said he needed to talk to me about something. But I still don't know why he wanted to talk to me. We didn't have a chance to get around to it."

"Do you think the shooter might have been aiming at Forrest and you got in the way?"

He stared at her and touched the bandage on his head again. "I have no idea."

"Well, you need your rest. Anything I can do to help, just let me know. I'll be around. Here's my card if you think of anything or need anything. I mean that."

He examined the card.

"HIT? Haines Insurance Training?"

"Yes, that's my company. I train insurance fraud investigators."

He gave her a long look. "You're an investigator?"

"Yes, well, not anymore. But I used to be for many years."

He looked back at the card.

"Have you farmed all your life?" she asked.

"No. I went to college, got a job as an agricultural manager at a big farm out west, then dad got sick so I came back and started working on the farm full-time. I really like it. He died and left it to me, so I just kept on farming."

"You the sole heir to the farm?"

He nodded. "I am. And I love it. I love farming." He suddenly looked drained.

"I see. Well, I'd better be going."

"Ms. Haines?"

"Please, call me Emma."

"Okay, Emma. About what my sister said about my cheating."

Emma looked at the floor.

"I just... Well, I didn't cheat on Tammy. I never even thought about it. That's all."

She looked at him, turned away, then faced him again.

"If you think of anything else that might help figure this thing out, I'd appreciate it if you'd give me a call."

She left him staring at her business card.

She climbed in her truck and pulled her phone from her purse and hit the number for Merek's cell.

"Hey, Miss H. What's up?" Merek finally answered after the sixth ring.

"Hey, Merek. Sorry to bother you on a Sunday."

"*Nie ma problemu.* You can double my pay this week."

"You should be a comedian, you know that? You in the middle of anything?"

"A nap."

"Well, can you wake up and do something for me?"

"*Pasjonujący*, Miss H."

"What? Never mind. I need you to do some research on some people down here in Chillicothe, the Mycon family. Two brothers named Alder and Forrest. A sister named Willow. Parents deceased. Owned a big family farm. Alder owns and farms it now. Check out his ex-wife, Tammy too. Call Joey tomorrow if you need to."

Joey Reed was a detective on the Clintonville police force and a good friend of Emma and Merek's. They'd solved many insurance fraud cases together over the years when she'd worked at Matrix and Joey was always ready to help them out.

"Charles and I witnessed a shooting on the water yesterday. Someone in the woods shot Alder, but luckily didn't do much damage. He and his brother, Forrest, were paddling in kayaks in front of us. You can read about it online on the Gazette's site. Can you do that and get back to me with the info?"

"Sure thing. That it?"

"For now."

"Okay. I gotta scram." He ended the call.

Emma smiled and shook her head. If Merek had one flaw, it was that he never said goodbye; he was always too busy 'scrammin'.

She hit 411 and asked for the number of Tammy Mycon, but there was no listing.

"She must've remarried or changed her name," Emma said to herself, sliding her phone back in her purse. She put the truck into gear and pulled out of the hospital parking lot.

The smell of cooking wafted from the kitchen as Emma walked into the dining room of the bed and breakfast. Robert was whistling when she tapped on the kitchen door.

The kitchen was cozy and decorated with a green leaf theme. There was a large pan of something in the oven of the old-fashioned gas stove. Robert looked up from chopping cucumbers on a cutting board.

"Emma, it's so nice to see you. How's your day going?"

"It's okay, I guess. I went to visit Alder in the hospital and his siblings came in, Forrest and Willow. I see your point about her. She's quite the character, as is Forrest. It's almost impossible to believe they're related to Alder."

Robert nodded and continued chopping. "I try to avoid her whenever I see her coming. That woman has a terrible temper. She screamed at me once for reaching for the same box of Cheerios. I suppose I would be foul too if I was in her shoes. Rumor has it she's in debt up to her eyeballs and has to deal with the fathers of those children, whom I might add, aren't the most upstanding citizens in the community. In fact, two are no longer around. One's in prison and one left town soon after he donated his, uhm, how should I say it, services to her." Robert wrinkled his nose.

"She didn't look like she shopped for clothes too

often."

Robert smiled. "If she shops, I doubt it's for external beauty. Most of her purchases, I hear, are for internal gratification."

"Drugs?" Emma asked, leaning against the wall, crossing her arms.

Robert nodded. "Forrest too. But, that probably doesn't come as any surprise to you, with your background."

"Doesn't surprise me in the least. Sad for the kids, though. Can someone do something for them?"

"No, not really. She maintains as a mother. The children are fed, appear healthy and happy, and clothed. That's what people see when she takes them out in public, which is seldom. Do you have any brothers or sisters, Emma?"

"No. I guess my parents threw away the mold when they saw me. Didn't want any more of *that*."

They laughed.

"Well, you're probably not missing much. Just more gifts to buy at Christmas and family bickering. I have four sisters and two brothers. Often, it can be cumbersome. But we're always there for one another when we need to be and I wouldn't have it any other way."

"That's nice. I have Charles and Mary. And Murray."

"Ahhhh, Murray. How is that adorable basset hound? You're welcome to bring him here again anytime. We are pet-friendly, you know."

"I should've brought him, I guess. He and Alexander got along pretty well the last time."

"Alexander can take care of himself. He just goes and hides someplace when other animals are here."

Just at that moment, Alexander came slithering around the corner and meowed, waving his long tabby tail.

"So, did you find out anything from Alder about who might have shot him?"

"Not from Alder, but Forrest and Willow insist it's his ex-wife, Tammy. Know anything about her?"

Robert chuckled. "Tammy? Tammy Eastland? Yes, I know a great deal about her."

"So, she remarried. I figured she might have."

"Yes."

"I'm all ears," she said.

"Tammy Eastland is a lovely woman and an outstanding citizen. She's on my church board and creates the Sunday bulletin. She often helps me cook here, right in this kitchen, for church events. And she would not go sneaking through the woods to shoot her ex-husband. "

"Well, Forrest and Willow claim she's out for revenge since Alder cheated on her."

Robert smiled. "Tammy? Revenge?" He chuckled and shook his head. "Very doubtful. I've known her and her family for years, even through her divorce. Oddly enough, it was one of the calmest, most amicable divorces I've ever heard of. From what I understand, there were no ill feelings between them when they split." Robert slid chopped cucumbers into a large bowl, picked up two more and started peeling them into the red enamel sink.

"So why'd they split?"

"Oh, Emma, who's to say? She alluded to me that they simply fell out of love."

"How long after the divorce did she remarry?"

"Six months. Clara and I catered the wedding. They're a lovely couple."

"Six months? That's pretty quick."

He nodded.

"Who'd she marry?"

"Taylor Eastland."

"Eastland. Eastland. I've seen that name around here. Why?"

"Probably because he is the largest realtor and homebuilder in the area, if not the county. Eastland Realty. In fact, Taylor sold me this place."

"You know, sometimes I miss being in a small town, and others…"

"Yes, I know what you mean. Well, any place you live has it's good and bad points."

"I can't argue with you there. So, what's Tammy do?" "She's Taylor's office manager. And a very efficient one, I'm sure. She's also a realtor."

"Ahhh, the family business. Was she having an affair with Taylor? Six months; sure seems like a quick marriage."

Robert dumped more cucumbers into the bowl and picked up three tomatoes and began slicing and chopping. He shook his head. "I don't believe so. Of course, she knew Taylor, but I don't think she has it in her, or him either, to have had an affair. Taylor is much older than Tammy. She's in her twenties and he's, I believe, nearly sixty-three. He's a well-respected businessman in the community."

Emma smiled and took a deep breath. "Wow. Good for ole' Taylor! It happens to the best of us, that's for sure. Maybe Tammy and I have something in common."

"Oh?"

Emma looked out the window then back at Robert. "I've been seeing an older gent myself. I met him while Charles and I were kayaking in West Virginia about four months ago."

"Emma, this *is* big news. This isn't like you. I've never known you to be impressed by any man, let alone say you're seeing him. Well, let me hear all about this *older gent."*

Emma smiled. "Well, let's see. I met him while Charles and I were kayaking in West Virginia this past July. He's a widower and has two grown kids who are both surgeons, and four grandkids. They all live in New York City. He's a retired reporter and editor from *The New York Times* and now he lives in West Virginia, and owns the town's newspaper—*The Stonefalls Post.* He has a wonderful, yet very old and wacky secretary named Rhonda, who reminds me of an older Marge Simpson. Anyway, he's tall, with thick gray hair, extremely handsome, loves kayaking and hiking, and has a gorgeous house on a mountainside with a big golden retriever named Maggie. Best of all, we really have fun together."

"And, what's this gent's name?"

"Stratton. Stratton Reeves."

"And?"

"And — that's about it. I've been down there and stayed at his place, and he's stayed at mine."

"When are you going to bring *Mr. Stratton Reeves* here and leave Charles at home?" He winked at her. "Oh, I'm kidding. Bring them both."

She laughed. "Well, Charles may be getting pretty booked up himself. He's been seeing someone, too."

Robert lifted a head of lettuce from the sink and resumed chopping.

"Now that *is* big news. I never thought he'd see anyone again after Simon broke that man's heart. I remember him staying here for several days. All he did was sit in the great room and stare out the window. Frankly, he worried me."

"Me, too. I don't think he'll ever be completely over Simon, but at least he's trying."

"Well, good for both of you." Robert tidied up the counter and turned to Emma, wiping his hands on a towel.

"Emma, I'd really love to chat with you more, but I have a luncheon to cater. If you'd like, I can leave you something here to eat."

"That sounds great, Robert. Thanks. Oh, just one more question."

Robert looked at her.

"Does Tammy drive a red Jeep Liberty?"

"Yes, she does. Why?"

"Oh, just curious."

After having eaten the marinated steak salad that Robert had left for her, Emma sat on the window seat in the parlor. She'd been reading her Kindle and glancing out the window now and then to look at the beautifully landscaped yard. Leaves fell and tumbled over the tops of the last of the large bed of Black Eyed Susans that swayed in the breeze. *It won't be long before fall will lose the battle to winter and snow will start flying,* she thought.

Just as she decided to go upstairs and grab a quick nap, her cell, which sat beside her leg, began to ring.

"Hey, Merek."

"Hey, Miss H. I got the information on the Mycon family.

"Okay, hold on." She walked to the dining table where her purse hung on the back of a chair. She retrieved her notebook and pen. "Okay, shoot."

"I called Joey and he was in his office today, so I didn't feel so bad about doing this on a Sunday for you. But he said you owed him a dinner at The Wildflower."

"Ahhh, that Joey. He works too hard. He'll get his

dinner and you'll get an extra hundred in your paycheck. Now, what do you have?"

"Alder Mycon inherited the family farm two years ago; just him. His brother and sister were purposely and clearly not to inherit anything. It's about twelve hundred acres on Sarsaparilla Road. Has about a quarter million dollars worth of mineral and timber rights combined too. He went to Chillicothe High School, graduated with an agriculture science degree from Ohio University. Married Tammy Karsonly in June of 2005 and they divorced in December 2010. No kids.

"She's twenty-six, graduated Chillicothe High School, also went to college at Ohio University and graduated with honors with an accounting degree. Homecoming queen in high school and college. She's a real hottie from her Facebook and website pictures. Very good-looking lady indeed. She married again, a realtor in Chillicothe, name of Taylor Eastland, in June 2010 and got her realtor's license. I have his company report from his bank. He's doing very okay."

"How very okay?"

"*Zamożny*. Guy is worth about three million, no money troubles, runs it straight up. Been in business since he was thirty-years old. Owns his house, built it himself. No mortgage. Never been married. No kids, except his wife. He's sixty-one. Sound familiar?" Merek laughed.

Emma was forty-four and Stratton was sixty-four.

"Well, yay for Taylor. Can't wait to meet him, especially after meeting Alder. That kid's a hunk."

"Now, Miss H. Mr. Stratton would be jealous."

Emma smiled. "What about Alder's finances?"

"Nothing bad. No debt except a truck payment and a new tractor." He rattled off the license plate of the truck and make of the tractor. "Both financed with Chillicothe Bank and Savings. Both loans taken out about a year ago. All payments are on time. Guy's clean."

"Okay. What else?" Emma jotted notes.

"Forrest Mycon is a loser. In and out of jail many times. So far, just the normal small stuff. Drunk and disorderly, disturbing the peace, three DUIs, busted for pot. Three ex-wives, last divorce was ten years ago. No children on record.

"Willow has five kids, all under ten. Married and divorced one of the fathers, never married the others. She must be a busy lady. Never graduated high school and no job record, gets welfare checks every Wednesday."

"Hmm... Anyway, anything else?"

"Oh, just one thing I saved to mention lastly."

"And what's that?"

"Tammy was the best sharp shooter on her rifle team in high school and college. Won several competitions. Made a small feature story in *Sports Illustrated* while she was in college, her picture was on the cover."

"That is interesting. What's she drive?"

"A 2010 red Jeep Liberty and her husband owns a new black Ford truck." He gave her the plate numbers.

Merek's doorbell chimed over the airwaves.

"Anything else?"

"No, Miss H. That is all. Hey, I need to scram." And with that, the phone went silent.

Merek placed his Samsung smartphone on his walnut and glass coffee table and crossed the expansive living room, walking in front of the glass-wall that overlooked the Olentangy River. He opened his apartment door and Ludnella Czerwinski strutted in, wearing skin-tight leather pants and red patent leather stilettoes. There was a Reed Krakoff bag slung over her thin shoulder, a gift from Merek. The silver rings in her ears, nose and eyebrows, and sequined halter top under her black leather biker's jacket glittered in the light of Merek's lamp as she turned and kissed him. They kept their lips locked as she dropped her bag and jacket on the leather sofa and made their way to his bedroom, moaning occasionally and removing each other's clothes.

Three hours later they lay naked in Merek's king-sized bed. Her head was on his chest as she gently traced her gold fingernails up and down his stomach. She moved her head to better situate her waist-long white hair and the line of hoop earrings that surrounded her lower and upper right ear.

They'd met at the dry cleaners where she worked six months ago when Merek was picking up Emma's dry cleaning. Since then, they'd been riding their Harleys together and spending a great deal of time in and out of Merek's bed.

"Did you tell her?" she asked him in Polish.

Merek stared at the ceiling for several seconds.

"*Nie.*"

"Why not?" she jerked away.

"I am not sure about moving to Colorado, Ludnella."

"But I thought you wanted to go live in the mountains with me?" She kissed his stomach.

He squirmed.

"Miss H. treats me very well and pays me a lot of money and I like it here," he answered her in Polish.

Ludnella sat up and propped her head on her elbow. "Miss H. Always Emma Haines. But you can never be away from her in case she *needs* something. She is using

55

you. She is no good for you." Ludnella poked a long, gold-painted fingernail into Merek's chest.

He said nothing. Finally he said, "I will think about it more."

She kissed him and slowly pulled away. "Merek, I love you, but I will go with you or without you. I have been in Ohio too long. I came from Poland, like you, to see America. I have not seen everything I want to see and you said you have not either.

"You said, just the other day, that you wanted to come with me and now you are not sure? It is the money. It is the love of money that stops you. You are becoming too Americanized. You are losing your spirit to the money. And you are nothing but a slave to Emma Haines; nothing but a Polock slave to her."

Merek gave her a look and turned away.

"You listen to me, Merek. You must jump whenever your phone rings. Just like today. It is Sunday. And she calls you to work. What if we'd been out riding in the beautiful woods? Would you have had to come back here to do her research? Why cannot she do her own research? I tell you, you are nothing but her Polish slave, Merek."

"That is not true. She does not own me. And if we had been riding, I could've done most of the research on my Samsung, as long as I had reception. What you say is wrong."

Ludnella hurriedly got out of bed and went into the bathroom, slamming the door behind her.

Merek swore in Polish, rolled onto his side and pulled the blankets over his head. Did he love Ludnella enough to leave his life, his job, his penthouse apartment, and his friends, including several other blondes he enjoyed keeping company with now and then? He just wasn't sure.

But he was sure about one thing. He liked working

with Emma. They were a team. He'd watched a lot of television and movies when he first arrived in America and he and Emma were as good as any teams on TV. He was like Thomas, played by Sean Hayes, and Emma was like Edward, played by Jack Nicholson in the movie "The Bucket List." And he loved it. And, yes, there was the money.

Emma didn't treat him like a slave, but as an equal partner in the company. They'd even talked about him becoming an official partner someday. Ludnella just didn't understand.

The shower went on and he crawled out of bed and put on his silk robe. He walked into the kitchen and pulled sandwich fixings from the new stainless-steel refrigerator he'd just purchased.

As he made his sandwich, he hoped that Ludnella would leave. He didn't feel like continuing their argument. He just wanted to lie on his couch and watch television and eat in peace.

Twenty minutes later, Ludnella came into the kitchen, her heels clicking on the tile floor, her waist-long, blonde hair swaying around her waist.

Merek looked at her and immediately knew that yes, he did want to go away with her. Maybe he *was* in love with her. He walked around the bar counter, took her in his arms, and kissed her as hard as he could. She leaned into him.

He crooned and spoke into her neck in their native language. "I will talk to Miss H. soon, I promise. These things take time. You must understand. And you must admit, you like expensive things, my sweet. Do you not? Perhaps I can take a long leave and we can travel."

She smiled into his face. "We can still have expensive things and will be more happy on the road. We can live in the mountains and go to anyplace we desire, my darling. But it must be more than a long leave. I want you to marry me and we go away, for good. No more Miss H. Just you and me, my love."

He looked into her round hazel eyes and kissed her again.

# CHAPTER 5

Tammy Eastland lived in a house that a successful builder would have built; brick, big, on a huge lot, on a tall hill, behind a white picket fence, complete with grazing horses in the bottom field. She'd told Emma to stop by the house at one o'clock and go to the building behind it; the company office.

Emma pulled into a small paved lot behind the house. A white Ford Taurus sat in one of the spots. She got out and walked across the lot to a thick wooden door. An ornate, hand-painted "Open" sign hung on the front of it. She opened the door and went in.

A plump, happy woman sat behind the front desk. A name plate on the desk read Lori Eastland.

Lori looked nothing like Rhonda, Stratton's secretary. Rhonda was skinny, in her seventies, and wore mostly orange polyester pantsuits with matching plastic jewelry and enough perfume to choke a room full of people wearing gas masks. But she knew the newspaper business and Stratton had insisted she come with the deal when he bought it five years ago. Rhonda loved Emma for "making that man happy again."

Lori looked up from her keyboard with a sweet smile. "Hello, there. May I help you?"

"Hi, my name's Emma Haines. I talked to Tammy earlier today and she said to stop by at one."

"Oh, yes. She said you'd be stopping in. Just a moment, please."

She picked up the phone receiver from the phone on her desk. Her saggy upper-arm jiggled as she hit a button and announced Emma's arrival. "Just have a seat and Tammy will be right out."

"Thank you."

Emma sat in an overstuffed chair across the room. A few seconds later a door behind Lori opened. Merek was right. One of the most strikingly beautiful young women Emma had ever seen strolled out. She had a perfect white smile, a confident walk, a toned body, and long black hair. She wore a fitted pinstripe suit, hose, and black pumps. Totally professional.

"Hello, I'm Tammy Eastland. I'm so pleased to meet you. Ms. Haines? Is that right? Did I pronounce that correctly?" She shook Emma's hand.

"Yes. Please call me Emma. Thank you for seeing me on such short notice."

"Oh, that's not a problem at all. Well, Emma, let's just go into my office and I'm sure I can help you find exactly what you're looking for."

She thanked Lori as she passed by, leading Emma into her office, and gently closed the door behind her.

"Please, have a seat at the table."

Emma walked to a round conference table and sat down.

"May I get you something to drink? Tea, coffee, juice or water?"

Emma shook her head. "No thanks. I'm fine."

Tammy smiled and nodded. "Alright. Just let me know if you change your mind. Now, you said you know the Shaws and you're looking for a house?" Tammy said as she walked to the table.

"Yes. I'm staying at their bed and breakfast. A friend and I come here often to kayak and we've stayed there for years. We live up north, about an hour, in Clintonville, but I've been thinking about buying a place down here because I'm here so often. I love staying at First Capital, but you know, I wouldn't mind having my own place. You're a realtor. You understand."

Tammy nodded, sat down, crossed her long legs, and pulled down her skirt. "I certainly do understand and I'm sure I can help you."

"Robert mentioned to me that they bought their house from your husband and said the experience was wonderful. So, here I am and I'd like to work with you."

Tammy's face lit up like a spotlight. "How nice of him to refer you to us."

"Well, actually, they don't know I'm looking. I'm sure you understand. I do love it there. But, he spoke so highly of you and your husband and, well, that means a lot to me. Anyway, I'm sure you're booked today, but I wanted to meet you and talk to you about it while I'm in town."

"I'm so glad you did." She checked her watch. "I have an open house this afternoon in an hour. As a matter of fact, why don't you come and check it out. It's a nice little house. We can talk there, before people arrive. What exctly are you looking for?"

"I don't really know yet. Something small, with a fenced yard. I have a small, older basset hound, Murray. I'd like to have a place for him to roam outside, but not too big. Maybe downtown or out near Bourneville or even Bainbridge if you have any out that far. A double garage, doesn't have to be attached."

Tammy laughed happily and waved a left hand that was home to a huge diamond ring perched beside a circle of diamonds in a wedding band. Emma wondered if her arm ever got tired from hauling it around.

"We sell houses all over the tri-county area. I'm sure we can find you the perfect house."
"Good. Good."
"You say you go kayaking?"
"Yes. As a matter of fact, my friend and I were kayaking on Paint Creek yesterday and witnessed a shooting. You might have read about it in the paper this

morning or saw it on the news?"

"Yes. Why, yes. You're one of the people who were behind Alder? I did see it on the morning news. I remember hearing your name now." She sat back, looked at the floor, and frowned.

"Yes. Wait. You know Alder? Oh, now, wait. Tammy. You're Alder's ex-wife?" Emma smiled her warmest smile.

Tammy glanced up with a puzzled look. "I am. But, how did you know that?"

"Well, I went to see Alder at the hospital this morning. I wanted to see how he was doing and he happened to mention you when we were talking about family and, you know, just making conversation."

"Oh. I see. Well, what a coincidence."

"Why, yes it is. What is it they say? Seven degrees of separation or some such?" Emma laughed.

Tammy looked serious. "How *is* he doing? I can't believe he was shot. And you saw it happen?"

"Yes. I saw everything." Emma paused and watched Tammy closely.

"What happened?" she asked, looking genuinely concerned. If Tammy were hiding anything, she was good at it. But Emma had seen the best over her career.

Emma told her the public version about the shooting, leaving out the part about her chasing the shooter through the woods. The description of the shooter and the Jeep wasn't information that Day would've shared with the media and Emma knew better than to divulge it.

"It's all so terrible. Who would want to shoot Alder? He's one of the nicest men in the world. I know that."

"That's the million dollar question. Well, since you're related, I'm sure the Sherriff has been – or soon will be – around to ask questions like that, and more," Emma said, nonchalantly, looking around the neat office. Everything was in its place and looked new. A wedding picture of Tammy and an older man, probably Taylor, stood on an oak bookcase.

"We're not related. We're divorced. And they haven't been here."

Emma looked at her. She certainly didn't seem like someone who would drive a muddy Jeep, run into the woods, and try to shoot her ex-husband, but her experience as an insurance investigator had confirmed – you cannot judge a book by its cover. But, still... It just didn't feel right.

"Well, I can tell you, they'll be around. I worked as an insurance fraud investigator, with lots of cops on lots of different cases for twenty years. Now, I have my own business, training investigators. So I do know about that. They'll be questioning everyone that ever knew him about the attempted murder."

Tammy put her hands to her mouth. She looked like she might burst into tears, but composed herself. "When you put it that way, it sounds so horrible. But Alder and I haven't been married for almost a year. I've been married to my current husband since June."

"That's not very long ago. They'll probably go back many years and they'll want to know where everyone was yesterday during the time of the shooting."

"Well, I was *here*. I'm usually here. So is Lori. She was here too. We're here almost all Sundays too, after church. Real estate is a non-stop business and we're busiest on the weekends. And we're a family business. Lori's my husband's sister. All his brothers and sisters and some other people in his family work for Taylor, my husband. It's his business, well, ours now."

"That's good. It's a beautiful place."

"Thank you. We all work very hard."

"That's obvious. You've got signs all over town. I'll bet you're really busy. Selling lots of houses lately?"

"As a matter of fact, the market here is picking up. We've really been busy. I showed seven houses yesterday. The market's finally coming back."

Emma looked at her. "You showed seven houses yesterday, yourself?"

"Well, yes." Tammy smiled and nodded. "Seven. Like I said, I've been very busy."

"I thought you said you were here." Emma pointed to the floor.

"Well, when I said 'here' I meant working. I wasn't actually *here* in the office the entire day. When I show houses, I do a lot of my office work out of my car. I was so busy and one woman stood me up. That was frustrating, but it happens sometimes."

"I'll bet being a realtor is a hard job. People calling you at all hours with all kinds of questions, meeting all types of people."

"Yes, well, sounds like you would know about that too."

Emma nodded and raised her eyebrows. "That's for sure."

Tammy checked her watch. "You want to follow me over to the house? It's only about ten minutes from here. I believe it even has a fenced yard. It's on Lillian Street, if you're familiar with the area."

"Not sure where that is. I'll just follow you. Now if it's the house I want, wouldn't that be another crazy coincidence?"

"Why, yes. It certainly would," Tammy said, smiling, as she walked to a closet. She pulled out a blue, hip-length jacket, and slipped it on.

Emma could feel her core temperature rise.

"My car's out back. Just follow me."

Emma walked through the parking lot and climbed into her truck. As she turned the key in the ignition, Tammy waved and smiled as she passed, driving a shining red Jeep Liberty.

Emma pulled in behind Tammy in front of a small white Cape Cod house. She got out of her truck and tried to study the Jeep as much as she could without bringing attention to herself. Tammy stood on the sidewalk waiting for her.

"Go ahead and go on in. I need to make a quick phone call. I'll be right there," Emma yelled to Tammy, waving her to go in the house.

"All right." Tammy turned and went into the house as Emma pulled her cell from her purse and pretended to make a call, walking back toward her truck. When the door of the house closed behind Tammy, Emma walked closer to the Jeep. She went behind it, knelt and looked under it. She examined the rear license plate and the bolts and checked the back section of the Jeep, looking in as many nooks and crannies as she could, hoping Tammy wouldn't glance out a window and see her.

Emma stood, frowned, scratched her cheek, put her cell back in her purse and walked to the house. Nothing.

She went in the house and Tammy excitedly gave her a tour.

It was a nice house, but Emma wasn't interested in buying it. Or any other house for that matter. She loved her home in Clintonville; a small condo in a double unit off High Street within walking distance of her office, the Whetstone Library, and her favorite breakfast nook and Saturday-night-fried chicken-restaurant, The Wildflower Café. And she doubted she'd ever find another neighborhood that had a grocery store like her favorite, Weiland's Market on Indianola; with its fresh foods and friendly staff. She and Charles both loved shopping there. It was more than a grocery; it was a neighborhood gathering place where people ran into each other and chatted, attended wine and beer tastings, and bought unique and tasty food, much of it supplied by local producers. Emma especially liked that. She couldn't imagine living anyplace else.

While she talked with Tammy for about twenty minutes, she examined Tammy's blue jacket, hanging on the back of a kitchen chair. Not a speck of dirt or even a fabric snag.

A couple came in, eager to see the house. She and Tammy exchanged business cards before she left.

Emma gave the Jeep one last exam on her way back to her truck. Not a speck of mud or even dust for that matter. The Jeep, inside and out, looked immaculate. In the hatch area, two "Open House" signs were stacked on a small blanket. Tammy appeared to be the sort of car owner whom Charles would admire.

She got in her truck, shut the door, and sat staring at the Jeep before she called the Paintville Sheriff Department and asked for Day.

"I'm sorry, Detective Day is off on Sundays. Can someone else help you?"

"I really do need to talk to her. It's about yesterday's shooting. This is Emma Haines. I was one of the witnesses."

"Hold the line, please."

Some time passed before Day's voice came over the phone, followed by a click from the transfer.

"This is Sheriff Day. How may I help you, Ms. Haines?"

"I'm sorry to call you on a Sunday afternoon, but I had to talk with you."

"About?"

"You probably should question Tammy Eastland about the shooting. I was just at her office, claiming to need a realtor. I followed her to a house in her red Jeep Liberty while she wore a blue jacket. Her vehicle and jacket are both like the ones I saw yesterday. And you already know what she looks like."

Day took a deep breath and let out a long sigh.

"I just spoke with Tammy and her husband in church this morning and noticed her blue jacket like the one you described. And I also know she drives a red Jeep Liberty."

"Look, I figured you're probably friends or acquaintances and I don't think she's a woman who would shoot anyone, but that's not for me to decide. Just a gut feeling and in all my years as an investigator, my gut's rarely let me down. But, I hate to say, she *is* fitting the description."

"I know. You're right. She's an acquaintance and it's definitely disturbing. She and her husband are well-respected in the community."

"Well, there's something else too."

"What's that?"

"You may want to confirm that she was the best sharp shooter on her rifle team in college. She was even featured in *Sports Illustrated*."

Emma could hear Day's brain churning over that piece of information or maybe she already knew that too.

"The good news is that I didn't find a speck of mud on her Jeep and it would've been pretty hard to clean it all off from the way it was covered. Her blue jacket didn't have a spot or snag on it either. And if it was Tammy who did the shooting, Alder probably wouldn't be around to talk about it. She wouldn't have missed."

"Valid points."

"You haven't released my description of who I saw running through the woods to anyone yet, the press, Alder or his siblings? Anyone?"

"Ms. Haines, you being an investigator with your reputation and background know that information can't be released while we're looking for a suspect."

Emma smiled. Day had checked up on her, just like she knew she would. Emma liked her.

"Why are you asking?" Day said.

"I just wanted to confirm that I'm not leaking any information on the case either." She thought of telling her what Forrest had said, but decided against it. She needed to do some more digging on her own.

"Ms. Haines, based on what I know about you, I never doubted that you would even think about it. And your friend, Charles Wellington, has the highest security clearance I've seen in my fourteen years on the force. You two have quite impressive backgrounds."

"Thank you. Oh, and one more thing."

"Yes?"

"The kayaks that Alder and Forrest Mycon were paddling; what happened to them?"

"I had them picked up in another truck and Forrest loaded them at the station and took them in his truck when he left after we questioned him."

"Did you happen to run a background check on the tag numbers?" Ohio was one of eight states in the country that required registration of kayaks.

"No, we really didn't see a reason to. Why?"

Emma sighed. "I don't know. Just something about it all bugs me. Neither one of them have kayaked for years and yet Forrest shows up with a couple of pretty nice boats and gear. Any reports of stolen boats around?"

"No. But I'll check into it more. I like the way you think. Is there anything else?"

"Not right now."

"Look, I really do appreciate your help, but I'm curious why you're still here since you live in

Clintonville and have a business to run. And I don't need to remind you, you're not at liberty to be active in this investigation. You're not authorized or have permission. You know that."

"Yes. I know that. Let's just say I'm a concerned citizen, wanting to help out," Emma said.

Day said nothing for several seconds. "You will call me whenever you think of anything or discover anything, right Ms. Haines?"

"Yes. Absolutely. We're on the same side, right?"

Day laughed. "Yes. We're on the same side and I do admire you and your experience. And Detective Joey Reed speaks very highly of you."

"Joey? You know Joey?"

"Yes, I know Joey. He's a good cop." She paused. "We dated for a while before I married my husband. Let's just leave it at that."

"Right. Got it."

"Good. Is there anything else?" Day asked.

"No. That's it for now. But I'll keep in touch," Emma answered.

"That's good. Well, good-bye, then."

"Bye."

Emma ended the call with Day.

*Joey, Joey, Joey.* She wondered how many women Joey had dated. He was quite the ladies' man, for sure. She shook her head, smiled, and hit the number on her speed dial for Charles. It went straight to his voicemail.

"Just checking in. Hope you and Mary are having a good time. Tell her I'm looking forward to seeing her soon. Bye."

She hit the end key, dialed the bed and breakfast and Clara answered. After a few seconds, Emma jotted down Willow Mycon's address on her notepad before she keyed it into her Garmin.

# CHAPTER 6

Emma pulled into the dirt drive of a shack on Blueridge Road, about ten miles outside of Chillicothe. It looked like it had been through a war. It was beat up, siding missing, paint peeling, tar paper hanging off the sides, and the porch was listing to left. The yard of tall grass and weeds was littered with worn toys of every kind, shape, and size. A bed sheet hung over the front bay window and a small beagle was chained to the rusted stairs leading to the front door. The dog started barking and wagging its tail as it crawled out from under the porch.

She climbed out of her truck, shut the door, and started for the shack. "Hey, pup. Your mom home?"

The beagle looked like she would explode any second, giving birth to a belly full of puppies.

The answer came through the walls as Willow's voice screamed, "I told you a hundred times not to leave the damn cereal box on the table and you just keep doing it! Now the bugs are back. Stop crying or I'll give you something to cry about."

The answer was a small child's whimpering voice.

Emma cringed and knocked on the door. It rattled in the frame.

"Mom, there's a little brown-headed woman at the door."

Children screamed and ran through the house, along with a set of heavy steps coming toward the door. Emma stepped back and waited before she looked up into Willow's puffy, red face.

"What do you want?" she snapped, catching her

breath as if she'd run a race.

"I'd just like to talk to you about your brother, if that's okay."

Willow blinked and looked around outside, as if she were looking for someone.

"I don't really got to talk to you, do I? I done talked to the sheriff."

"No. But I thought you might be upset and want to talk to someone about it. I thought you could tell me a little more about Tammy, since you say that's who shot him. Just curious about your proof."

Willow looked at her blankly. "I don't need no proof. I knowed that's who shot him." She took a deep breath, turned around, and screamed something at the kids that Emma didn't care to remember.

"Look, my place ain't cleaned up for visitors. And I'm pretty upset and don't really want to talk about it. Really bothers me that she tried to kill my brother."

"Well, I can understand that. It bothers me too. That's why I thought you'd like to try and figure out who might have shot him, for sure that is. Discover some proof about who shot him. Maybe he was just in the wrong place at the wrong time–an accident, perhaps. Or someone was aiming at Forrest and missed."

"I thought you wasn't no cop or nothing."

"I'm not. Just a concerned citizen. Your brother seems like a nice guy. Thought I'd help your family. That's all."

"Well…"

The kids screamed in the background and Willow turned her head.

Emma said, "Look, I'd be happy to buy you lunch somewhere. That way might be easier for us to talk. Give you a break from the kids. Lunch wherever you want, on me."

Willow took in a sharp little breath, her eyes darted

71

around. "Well, I guess that'd be okay."

"Great. Here's my card. Call me in the morning on my cell and tell me where to meet you or I can come pick you up."

"How'd you know where I lived?"

"Google."

"Who's that?"

Emma didn't reply and started down the steps and toward her truck. She turned back to Willow. "Call me tomorrow. Have a nice evening."

Willow slammed the door.

Emma got into her truck and hit a number on her speed dial.

Stratton answered on the second ring. "Hey, sweetheart, where are you?"

"I'm sitting in my truck outside the home of a woman who doesn't know who Mr. Google is."

"What's that?"

"Never mind. Hey, I just wanted to let you know I probably won't be home for a while and why and what's going on." She told him about the weekend.

"Emma, you seem to have a tendency to—"

"I know what you're going to say. Attract people with guns on rivers, right?"

"Well, as a matter of fact, yes. Something like that. Why don't you go home. Or do you think the cops are involved in this cover-up too?"

"No, the sheriff down here is top notch."

"Well, then go home."

"Can't," she said.

"Or won't?"

Silence.

"How was Tim's concert?" Emma asked.

Stratton's grandson, Tim, was a violin protégé at his junior high school in New York City. Stratton had flown there Thursday night to see him perform and visit with his son, Glen, and his daughter, Ellen, and their families. Ellen was the same age as Emma, Glen was two years younger.

"You do what you need to do. I'll cancel our reservations for the theatre for Tuesday evening if you can't make it."

"Oh, I'm sorry about that. I forgot." She paused, took a deep breath, and closed her eyes.

"Emma, are you still there?"

"I was wondering, well, would you be interested in coming here?"

"To Chillicothe?"

"Yes. I have a big bed in a lovely room at the bed and breakfast and—"

Stratton chuckled. "I'll be there tomorrow."

"Okay. And bring your boat."

"I'm glad you called."

"Me too."

"I'll be there by ten," he said.

"I'll save you some coffee."

She ended the call and stared out the windshield, smiling, holding her phone to her chest. The little female beagle stared back and wagged her tail.

Emma watched the dog until she crawled under the porch. *So sad. Such a cute little dog tied to a trailer and about to have puppies.*

She thought of Murray and hit her speed dial for her dog sitter, Janet. After they'd exchanged greetings, she asked if Janet could keep the basset for a few more days. Janet was Charles's neighbor and full-time dog sitter. She kept Murray often and "the boys" nearly every weekday at her large ranch house.

Emma put the truck into drive and headed back to the First Capital Bed and Breakfast to settle in for the evening.

Charles and his mother sat at their regular table in the bar at the Worthington Inn. As usual, when Mary came in from a long trip, they'd have a nice dinner there and she'd stay with Charles for a few days, and then he'd take her home, only an hour's drive south to Circleville.

He finished his *Chopin* martini and put the glass down on the table with a thud. Mary sipped a Rusty Blade Gin martini with two blue-cheese stuffed olives.

Charles nodded toward Tom, the bartender, and raised his empty glass. Tom smiled and nodded.

They loved to eat at the Worthington Inn. The drinks and food were always superb. The atmosphere was peaceful and relaxing with a touch of class. The beautiful, large wooden bar, dating from around 1880, came from Stout's Drug Store in Parkersburg, West Virginia. It was moved in pieces and reassembled in the pub. Paintings of old-day Worthington, Ohio, hung on the walls.

"Two martinis in less than an hour? What's wrong, Charles?"

"Nothing. I've just had an intensely rough week. I told you I witnessed a shooting, but I didn't tell you that I also learned some disturbing news from Emma this weekend."

"Oh? More disturbing than witnessing a shooting? I can't imagine."

"Mother, Simon called her. He's in Clintonville."

Mary frowned and took a big swig of her martini. She placed the glass on the table, stared at it, and rubbed the stem.

"That is disturbing. What a cowardly bastard. Doesn't even have the courage to call you, instead, he calls Emma."

"She told him off and hung up on him."

"Good for her. That's my girl. What on earth did he say?"

The waiter, Jason, brought Charles's second martini and placed it in front of him. Charles thanked him before he took a long sip.

"I don't know. She said it was around ten in the evening when he called. She said she was so angry she wouldn't let him get a word in edgewise. All I know is he told her he was in town and asked about me."

Mary shook her head. "How do you feel about him?"

Charles stared into his drink.

"You still love him, don't you?"

He looked into his mother's green eyes. She was a striking woman for seventy-six. Spry, small, and always tanned. She reeked of sophistication. And why wouldn't she, being a world golf champion; a celebrity.

She'd been married once, to Charles's father, who had left them days after Charles was born. But Mary didn't care. Charles Wellington had not only left her and his son, he'd walked away from the family estate outside Circleville, Ohio. Mary loved it and stayed. When her attorney told her it was legally hers, she made additions, redecorated, and added an 18-hole golf course.

She reached over and patted his arm. "I only wish I could relate, honey. I've never been in love with a man for more than ten seconds. They're like golf balls to me. Set them up and knock them off the tee. Unlike my golf balls, I usually don't care to see them again."

Charles sighed deeply, leaned back in his chair and crossed his arms. "Yes, mother, anyone who can read is well aware of your romantic escapades."

The press had a heyday with Mary Wellington's love life. Most recently, she'd been caught coming out of a hotel in France with a married movie director, holding hands, only to have it splashed over every news media in the world. And, she laughed about it.

"I'm sorry, dear. But you really do need to move on and get over Simon Johnson. He's just trash; rich and handsome, to be sure, but heartless trash, nonetheless. He's proved that to you, yet again. I like Ron. You should focus all your energies on him."

Jason returned. Charles ordered his favorite, Beef Worthington, and Mary ordered the Sunday evening seafood special.

His cell buzzed. He grabbed it out of his pocket and stared at it. The number was "Unknown." His heart quickened.

"I have no idea who this is." He stood quickly and walked away from the table, toward the front of the restaurant.

Mary sat watching him. She hoped it wasn't Simon. She knew if she ever ran into Simon Johnson again, she'd crush him like a roach.

She watched her son pace in front of the couch beneath a replica print of Van Gogh's "Starry, Starry Night" with the Worthington Inn painted into the background.

When she was younger, she had wanted one child to experience motherhood and raise as her own—alone. But she hadn't meant to get pregnant by Charles's father and didn't want to be married or have a man around all the time. But Charles's father had insisted on getting married when he found out she was pregnant. No matter. She'd divorced him and gotten exactly what she'd wanted in the end.

She was so proud of Charles. He'd been an easy child to raise as he loved mathematics and had a genius IQ. She'd raised him all on her own, exactly as she'd planned. He was *her* son. The best clothes from Italy. The best food. The best chefs. The best nannies. The best school. And the best British tutor money could buy, Samuel James. He'd lived with them during Charles's school years until he left for college at Harvard. And what a gentleman and lover Samuel had turned out to be.

She raised her head, smiled, and sipped her drink as she looked at her son.

It nearly killed her when Simon had walked out on him. If it hadn't been for Emma, he might well have had a serious nervous breakdown. She'd stayed at his house for months, helping him move through the pain, taking him kayaking, hiking, and bicycle riding. Mary had been on the road, golfing, as usual.

Jason came over to Mary with another martini and placed it beside her half-empty glass.

"What's this?" she asked, smiling into his face.

"A man gave me this note and asked me to deliver it with this martini. He said not to do so until he left, so when he left, he nodded toward me when he walked out and now I'm delivering it."

"How sweet. Thank you." *Another adoring fan.*

She was used to a lot of attention, but it was usually signing a quick autograph or posing in a picture, smiling with a total stranger like they were best friends. She unfolded the paper and began to read.

Her eyes grew wide and she threw the paper on the table as if it was a tarantula and stared at it. Charles returned and sat down.

"A vendor wanted to let me know that he has to cancel a meeting. Nothing... Mother, what's wrong?"

Mary pointed at the note on the table. She lifted her half-full martini and finished it off in one gulp. Charles looked puzzled and picked up the note.

*"Mary. You look prettier than you do on TV. I've been following your success all these years and now we need to talk. C."*

"What is this piece of nonsense? A fan? Where did

this come from?" Charles asked her, looking around the bar.

"Get Jason back over here, immediately," she said, sitting ramrod straight in her chair.

Charles went to the bar and asked Tom to send Jason back to the table. Jason, smiling, arrived in a matter of seconds, looked at Mary and changed to a frown.

"Yes, Mrs. Wellington. Is something the matter?"

"Who gave you this note?" she demanded, pointing at it.

"He didn't give his name. He was sitting in the back of the restaurant, through that room," Jason pointed to the rear dining area, "drinking a rum and coke."

Mary turned to look into the room behind their table.

"What did this man look like?"

"He was older and rather frail and wiry-looking. He had on a brown polyester suit and work boots. A brown wool hat."

"Thank you, Jason. That'll be all." Mary was used to dismissing people and Jason left the table. She lowered her head and shook it slowly.

"Mother? Who was it?"

She raised her glass and emptied the drink and nearly slammed the glass on the table.

"It's your father, Charles. The bastard's back."

# CHAPTER 7

"Emma, come on. You're giving me a complex. I'm beginning to think you don't like me. I was hoping we could go out to dinner after you finished your presentation, that is if I ever get to see it," Calvin Nelson, head of the claims department at Matrix Insurance whined into Emma's ear from her cell phone.

She leaned back against her pillow, sipped her coffee, and looked at the ceiling of her room in the B&B.

"I don't like you. But you keep hiring me anyway. And, I have to tell you, Merek and I appreciate that. I'm sorry I had to postpone the presentation. I'll have Merek send it. I won't charge you... as much."

"You do great work. Now, all I want to do is take you to dinner to thank you for the great work you do, Emma. Come on. Whatdaya say? Just dinner."

"The same thing I say every time you've asked me before. No thank you, Calvin. You pay me quite well and I appreciate it."

"Well, I won't stop asking, you know. I'm in love with you. I have been for years, since the first time I saw you."

Emma rolled her eyes. "If you have any questions on the presentation, call Merek."

"Merek. Now there's a piece of work. Why don't you bag that tattooed, Polish biker freak and get a real office manager?"

"He is a real office manager. And he's *not* a freak."

"Hey, you and he aren't—"

"No. Even though it's really none of your business,

Merek and I are a business team. That's it. Besides, I'm old enough to be his mother."

"Doesn't seem to bother you dating men old enough to be your ole' man."

Emma smiled and looked over at Stratton who was lying in bed with his back to her, snoring softly. "Word gets around fast."

"Yeah, around here. What do you expect?"

"Hey, I gotta run, Calvin. Remember, call Merek."

"Yeah, yeah, yeah. You off on one of your *kayak trips* or something?"

"Or something. Good-bye, Calvin." She ended the call and placed her phone on the bedside table. She snuggled under the covers and wrapped herself around Stratton. He moaned, rolled over, and kissed her on the nose.

"I still can't believe you drove up here in the middle of the night," she said into his ear.

"Disappointed?"

"Hardly. But now I'm pretty tired. Didn't get much sleep last night."

"And you're blaming me for that?"

"Well, no one else kept me up all night. Now, how did you get in here again?"

"I told you, I called here right after you called me and talked to Robert. I took a gamble that you'd told him about me. I told him what I had planned and he left a door key and room key under the mat."

"My, my, my. A bit presumptuous on your part, don't you think? I'm going to have to have a little chat with Robert. You could've been a killer come to finish me off."

"I'll finish you off."

"Oh, yeah?"

"Yeah. Come here." He threw a leg over her and kissed her.

Calvin Nelson sneered as he tossed his cell phone onto his credenza, leaned back in his chair, and propped his size thirteen designer loafers on his office desk. He stared over his beach-ball belly at the toes of his shoes. He clasped his fingers, put them behind his bald head, and leaned back. He had short round legs and the edge of the chair bumped the desk. He caught himself before he nearly tipped backward.

He settled in and stared at the ceiling. He pictured Emma in that black suit she'd worn the last time she'd given a presentation to the board a month ago. He'd turned up the thermostat in the room about thirty minutes before the meeting in hopes that she'd take off her jacket, a neat little trick of his that a former business partner, Marvin, had taught him before he'd started at Matrix. Sadly, he'd had to part company with Marvin after he was sent to prison for embezzling. They'd worked well together, but Calvin had no intention of going down with his friend.

As people had filed into the room and began sweating, Emma mentioned being a little warm and slipped out of her jacket and placed it on the back of a chair. He remembered being mesmerized by the muscles in her tanned arms and calves and the way she'd floated around the entire board room with such grace and confidence in those high heels. That shining brunette hair and that white smile. Her long sparkling necklace and matching earrings caught the light as she moved around the room, explaining the claims center's increase in closed calls. Her presentation had made his team look stellar. Old man Matrix had even given Calvin a smile and a nod from across the table; something the old geezer never did.

He smiled. He'd get rid of Mr. Matrix and the old fart with whom Emma had taken up company, soon enough.

His office phone buzzed. "Damn it." He pushed back from his desk, dropped his feet to the floor and hit the intercom button.

"What?" he snapped.

"I'm sorry to bother you, Mr. Nelson, but your standing Monday morning staff meeting began ten minutes ago. People are waiting, sir."

"Let 'em wait. Be good for them. Get their lazy blood flowing better. I'm in charge, not them. Tell them I'm on a call with Mr. Matrix. That'll shut 'em up."

"Yes, sir. Thank you sir."

He clicked off and stared at his computer monitor. He moved the mouse to his first bookmark. He clicked on the link and Emma's picture appeared on her H.I.T. website. He leaned back and stared at it.

He sighed. "Emma. Emma. Emma Haines."

After several seconds, he closed the web browser, stood, sucked in his gut and buttoned his jacket. The button looked as if it would shoot off at any second. He strolled out of his office, his jacket tail flaring open in the back as he formed a plan in his fat, bald head to get Emma Haines back at Matrix and keep her there and in his life—where she belonged.

At ten-fifteen Emma's cell buzzed. She rolled over and answered.

"'Lo," she mumbled into the phone.

"Emma, where are you?" Charles asked.

"In bed."

"In bed? Are you ill?"

"No, just really tired. Sleeping in. I don't do it often, so…What's up?" She sat up and rubbed her face.

"Emma it's late. Why on earth are you, of all people, still in bed?"

"What's up, Charles?" She rolled over and lay on her back.

"Emma, it's Mary."

She sat up in bed. "Mary? Charles, what happened?"

"Nothing, I mean, it's not really Mary. It's, well, it's my father."

"Your what?"

"My father. Seems he's in town."

Emma sat taller, pulling the sheet up to her neck. "What?"

"Yes. It appears he may be stalking her. First Simon calls you and tells you he's here and now this. When it rains, it certainly does pour."

"What? What's going on up there?"

"You tell me." He told Emma about the note Mary received at dinner the night before. "And, he just called her. He would like to meet with her *and* me."

"Wow, this is really huge."

"It most certainly is really huge. I'm a nervous wreck. I've never met the man. I'm not even sure I want to. Jason, our waiter, told us he was dressed wearing *polyester*. My father wearing *polyester*? Emma, that's simply preposterous."

"Well, you certainly don't take after your father, that's for sure. What do you want me to do?"

"Nothing. I just needed to talk to you about it, that's all. And, maybe you could ask Merek and Joey to look into his background. I'd do it, but I won't use my security clearance to snoop around like that. Besides, you're better at it. It's odd him showing up like this."

She yawned. "Sure thing. No problem."

"Emma, are you sure you're not ill?"

Stratton rolled over beside Emma. "Oh, I'm sorry, honey. I thought you were talking to me."

"Is that *Stratton*?"

Emma didn't answer. She smiled and mouthed "Charles" toward Stratton. He nodded and rolled back over.

"When did he... Oh, I *see*. Well, I'll certainly not keep you."

"Hey, I'll call you later. I think we may take a quick run down the Paint this afternoon and check out the crime scene, if we get around to it."

"Oh, Emma. Just stay in bed." The phone went dead.

Emma put the phone back on the side table, burrowed under the covers, and put her arms around Stratton. "Charles just gave me some very good advice."

After she and Stratton had gotten out of bed, she'd called Merek and asked him to check out Charles's father. Later, she and Stratton loaded their boats and gear and followed each other to Paint Creek, leaving her truck at Blain and taking Stratton's pickup to the Twin Bridges put-in.

"Robert and Clara are wonderful hosts, aren't they?" Emma asked as they paddled past the first bend and Little Copperas Mountain.

"That they are, indeed. The lunch was delicious," he said, gently paddling downstream.

"Yes. They normally only serve breakfasts, but they feed Charles and me every meal, no extra charge."

They'd been paddling for about forty-five minutes when they came around the bend at the bottom of Copperas Mountain.

"This is where the shooting took place. I'd like to take a look around in the woods. May take me a little while," she said.

"I'm in no hurry, sweetheart. Rhonda is holding down the office. I told her I would probably be away for a few days. Oh, she sends her love."

"Ahhh, Rhonda. What a wacky and wonderful woman."

Stratton nodded. "That she is."

They pulled their kayaks up on the shale bank below the road.

The hillsides were beautiful, displaying their assorted colors and textures below a clear blue sky with white, fluffy clouds floating above them; another perfect fall day.

They took off their life jackets and tossed them and their paddles into their kayaks. Stratton pulled out a metal bottle of water from his kayak and took a long drink. Emma drank from the red metal water bottle given to her by her friend, Sue Robinson, several years ago. She considered it such a good-luck item that she always carried it in her boat.

She detested the use of plastic water bottles; there were too many floating throughout the country on the many rivers she'd kayaked over the years.

"People don't realize how they need to keep themselves hydrated in cooler weather," Emma said, twisting the cap back on the bottle.

"True," Stratton replied and replaced his bottle back in his boat and stood, surveying the area. "This place is simply amazing." He looked around. "So, explain to me what happened."

Her brunette pony tail bobbed as she nodded.

"Well, Charles and I were paddling and we came around the bend back there and saw two men in kayaks in front of us, up there about twenty yards." She pointed.

"Wait. Let me back up to the beginning. When Charles and I were unloading our boats back at the put-in, that's where we saw the red Jeep Liberty covered in mud from bumper to bumper, even the license plates were covered in mud. You couldn't help but notice the thing. You could barely tell what color it was. There was also a beat up blue pickup.

"Anyway, I figured at least one of the men drove one of the vehicles. Later on I found out that the blue pickup was Forrest Mycon's, the brother who didn't get shot, and the red Jeep was what the shooter escaped in, and it's just like Tammy's."

Stratton put his hands on his hips and looked around. "Okay, I'm with you so far."

"So, Charles and I came around the bend," she pointed upstream, "and the shot came from over there, in the woods and hit Alder Mycon, shaved his forehead. Another sixteenth of an inch and the man's head would've been blown off. Lucky boy."

"Just one shot?"

Emma nodded. "Yes."

"Okay," he said as he turned, taking in the scenery. "Go on."

"Charles paddled down there to tend to Alder and propped him against that tree," she pointed, "while I paddled over there to the the woods. I saw something blue and black, moving away from the bank. It was the shooter, running away."

"Emma, darling, you have an uncanny habit of chasing people with guns when you're not armed. Very worrisome for me, I might add. We'll need to discuss that."

Emma scowled at him and continued. "Anyway, I

ran after the person who had long, black hair and was wearing a blue jacket."

"A woman?"

"So it seems, based on what Forrest and the sister, Willow, are claiming. They say it's Alder's ex-wife, Tammy Eastland. But, I'm not buying it. I'm not buying it at all, no matter what the evidence says."

"Why not?"

"I went to see Tammy Eastland. She's not the type of woman who would take a pot-shot at her ex-husband. I don't care if she does own a red Jeep Liberty like the one I saw or that she was an expert sharp-shooter on her college rifle team or owns a blue coat, like the one I saw on the shooter. Plus, during the time the shooting took place, she was out showing houses. She's a realtor. She doesn't have a motive to shoot Alder. I've checked it out. Well, okay, I had Merek check it out. Tammy's sitting pretty with her new hubby and she and Alder seem on amicable terms."

"What else did Merek find out?"

"That Tammy Eastland divorced Alder Mycon in 2010 and remarried six months later. Taylor Eastland is an older, rich realtor, and after they married, Tammy became a realtor too. They work in his family business with Taylor's brothers and sisters. This is Taylor's first marriage, no kids."

"That he knows of," Stratton said.

"Right. On record, anyway."

"Tammy and Alder have any kids?"

Emma shook her head. "No. They were married about five years, but no kids."

"Taylor have a reason to shoot Alder?"

"I don't know, but I intend to dig into that."

She put her hand along the edge of her ball cap and looked across the river. "I'm going to go through there again while we're here. I'll be back in a while."

"That's fine. I'll just walk down this road and admire the scenery. I feel like I'm out West, in Utah or Idaho someplace." He looked up the side of Copperas Mountain. "This is just truly *amazing*."

Emma nodded and looked up too. "It's awesome, isn't it? You may want to watch for the eagles. Charles and I saw two Saturday."

"I'll do that," he said.

She put her life jacket on, got into her kayak, and paddled across the creek to the west, pulled her boat on the bank, and tossed her paddle and life jacket in the boat. She looked around the woods, trying to find the same path she'd taken to chase the shooter on Saturday. It wasn't hard to see the broken twigs and smashed leaves.

She examined every twig as well as the ground. Nothing but leaves, leaves, and more leaves. The woods were quiet except for a nuthatch making its yink-yink sound above her in a dead tree, as it hopped head-first down the side of it. She watched the small bird jump down to another branch and begin pecking on the bark. It flitted to a small twig above Emma's head where she noticed what she thought was a spider web floating in the breeze. Giving it a closer look, it was a strand of long, black hair.

"Bingo," Emma said, as she gently removed the hair from the branch and placed it in a plastic baggie she pulled from her pocket.

"Thanks, little nuthatch."

A "yink-yink, yink-yink" came from the bird before it flew to another tree.

"Stratton! I found black hair on a branch over there," she yelled as she paddled toward him. He was bobbing in his kayak in an eddy along the side of the stream.

"Do you think it's the shooter's?"

"Yes. I'll overnight it to Joey and have him test it. If he can pull the DNA, Tammy could be in a whole lotta trouble."

"True. You going to call Day?"

"Not until I get the results. No sense in stirring up the pot for nothing."

"Isn't that called withholding evidence, Ms. Haines?"

"It is," she said, picking up her paddle and positioning her boat alongside his.

"Is this something you're known for? Withholding things?"

Emma paddled around a strainer. Once Stratton got around it, she paddled beside him again.

"Do I suspect a hidden question in your question, Mr. Reeves?"

"I don't know, do you?"

"Do you think I'm withholding something from you?"

"Well, I'd like to know how you feel about me because I'm in love with you."

"Whoa. Now that's pretty direct, as I've learned, you are."

"So?"

"So what?"

"Emma, let's not play games. We're adults. I'm a sixty-four-year-old man and you're a lovely forty-four year old woman who, I might add, is quite a babe."

"Really? Me? A babe?"

"Absolutely. The babe I'm in love with."

They paddled in silence for a few long seconds.

"Eeeeeerrrrrrrrrreeeee. Eeeeeeeerrrr. Eeaaarrrrr."

"What the hell was *that*?" Stratton asked. "A peacock?"

They looked up the hillside into a stand of red maples, leaves fluttering in the breeze.

"Yes, I think it was. I've heard them downstream, but never up here," she said.

"They sound like a woman screaming," he said. "What are they doing in the woods here?"

"Probably strayed from a farm around here. I worked on a case at Matrix; a stolen tractor claim. The farmer told me that his peacocks made great watchdogs and ate lots of bugs. So I asked him, 'If they're such great watchdogs, how did your tractor get stolen?' Ended up I questioned him for so long, he finally broke down crying and told me he hid it in a friend's barn and filed the claim because he needed the money. I felt sorry for him, but it was fraud and it had to be dealt with. Sad though. He'd just fallen on some bad times; drought, bills, then too much rain. He couldn't even use the tractor to plant. Farmers work so hard and deserve a lot more respect. They feed us, for crying out loud."

"They certainly do."

They paddled in silence before the peacock yelled through the woods again.

"The males are such beautiful birds. I always thought it sort of funny that human females are the *pretty ones* and in the animal kingdom, many times, it's the males that are the *pretty boys*." She looked at him. "Except for you. You're a *pretty boy*."

He laughed. "Hummph. A pretty *old* boy."

She laughed and paddled past him, putting distance between them.

## CHAPTER 8

Emma and Stratton sat opposite each other at the dining room table drinking their coffee. They'd just shared the Tuesday morning *Chillicothe Gazette* over breakfast and Stratton had moved on to *The New York Times*. Clara and Robert were in the kitchen. The sound of their voices, laughter, and dishes clattering floated through the air.

"I really do like this place," Stratton said to Emma, placing his paper on the table and glancing around the room.

"I do, too. Charles and I have been coming here for years. It's so homey. I despise hotels."

"Why's that?"

Emma shrugged. "I like cozier places to stay. Hotels are so cold and sterile. I've stayed in the best ones in the world. They're all pretty much the same to me."

Stratton placed his cup on its saucer and sat up straight. "Emma, speaking of hotels, I'd like you to spend a month with me in Europe, right now. We can stay in bed and breakfasts the entire time." His eyes were wide and bright and his smile covered his face.

She stared at him over her coffee cup. "I have a business to run."

Stratton crossed his arms in front of his chest, dropped his chin, and frowned at her. This was the fatherly look which Emma hated. "And I don't? Anyway, Merek runs your business."

"That's cold."

"That's true."

"Well, yeah. But I deliver the goods. And you have

Rhonda, so you can't talk."

He nodded. "I agree. So we're both in a very good position to be able to come and go as we please, so you have no excuses not to come to Europe with me. Or do you?"

She didn't say anything.

"Does your silence mean you won't go?"

"No. It means I need some time to think about it. Why do you want to go to Europe?"

"Ever been there?"

"Yes, several times."

"So you know how beautiful it is."

"Yes."

"So what's stopping you?"

Her cell rang in her purse that hung on the back of her chair. She dug it and her notebook and pen out quickly.

Stratton turned and looked out the window.

"Hey, Merek."

"Hey, Miss H. I have data on Charles's father."

"Great, hold on." She flipped to a blank page in her notebook and scribbled *Charles-Father* at the top. "Go ahead."

Merek told her Charles's dad was born and raised in Circleville, Ohio, and grew up on the family estate where Mary now lived. It had been in the family for four generations, but interest had waned about the property since the time of Charles's grandparents and father. They'd all moved to California and Mary took legal title to the large farm about fifty years ago.

Emma thought of all the fun she and Charles had at Mary's over the years, cooking out on her huge patio and deck and the fabulous dinner parties Mary liked to throw.

She had a flashback to Charles's fiftieth birthday party, nearly eight years ago, drinking the best champagne while they sat on the patio of the estate, the sun setting, a burnt orange in the western September sky. She remembered how Charles and Simon linked arms as they made a toast together, smiling happily at each other. She suddenly felt very sad and heavy, like someone had just dropped wet cement on top of her. "What else?" she said, snapping herself back to the moment.

"He lives in a small town called St. Hills twenty miles outside L.A. He does not own a car or a home. They were both repossessed about four years ago, after he lost his job as a janitor at a large computer software company. Looks like they closed, it was not because he was a bad worker. He is renting a room in a boarding house. No savings or retirement funds, about two-thousand in a checking account, lives on Social Security and a pension, and that's it."

Emma frowned as she continued to write. Could Charles, his father, and Mary be more different types of people? She thought of the Mycon family. "That's odd. If he had such a great job, he has no savings? No 401K? Nothing more?"

"He withdrew everything about three years ago."

"And his parents' house in California?"

"They sold it and moved into assisted living where they used all the money. May be where the son's money went too. The son got nothing when they died."

"Hmmm…. That it?"

"Well, I thought he may not be a healthy man and used the money for health reasons."

"Why's that?"

"I researched the bus company in the area, called and talked to the driver. For the past year, he has been getting off at a stop in front of a hospital three days a week."

"Hospital?"

"Yes. The local cancer center."

Emma stopped writing and closed her eyes. "Treatments?"

"No. He gets off there at 7:30 in the mornings and gets back on at four in the afternoons. Then, I called the hospital. He volunteers there. That's about everything I could find on him. He's clean. Just down on his out."

*Well, at least he and Charles had something in common — a big heart,* she thought. Charles volunteered at several community charities and donated heavily to the local Labrador rescue.

"Down on his luck, Merek. Down on his luck or down and out. So, how'd you get the bus driver to spill the info?"

"I have my ways, Miss H. Hey, I gotta…"

"Scram. I know. Bye."

She ended the call and smiled at the phone. *That Merek. He's something else. I need to give him a bonus,* she thought.

She started to talk to Stratton, but he was still looking out the window, clearly miffed. She hit the speed dial for Charles and relayed the information.

"So he's broke. Just as I suspected," Charles said.

"Appears that way."

"And why is that? He basically walked away from the estate in Circleville. He and his parents both did. It's all so confusing."

"Oh, Charles. Life is confusing. We know that."

"True. Well, thank you. This is helpful. I have to run. We'll talk later. Oh, and thank Merek for me."

"No problem. It's what we do."

"And quite well, I might add."

"Why, thank you, Charles. Talk to you later."

"Goodbye."

Stratton gave Emma a quizzical look when she put her phone and notebook on the table. While she told him about Charles's father, Clara came into the room carrying two plates with white cupcakes on each one. She set them on the table in front of them, along with two napkins.

"These are fresh from the oven. I have to cater a wedding reception today and I tried a new recipe. I need some guinea pigs. Robert likes them, but as he likes everything I bake, I need a more objective opinion." She stood back, smiled, wiped her hands on her apron, and gestured for them to try the cupcakes. "Go on. I don't have all day."

"I'm so stuffed, Clara. Really, I don't think I could eat another bite," Emma said.

"Then split one," Clara said.

"Alright," Stratton said. "Anything to help out."

"What a fine man you have here, Emma," Clara said, with a teasing tone, patting Stratton on the shoulder.

"He'll do, I guess."

Stratton gave Emma a 'so-there' look. Clara went to the cupboard, pulled out a butter knife, and handed it to Stratton. He removed the star decoration from the white icing, cut the cupcake in half, put half on the other plate, and handed it to Emma. "Do you cater many weddings?" he asked between bites.

"Oh, my, yes. At least a dozen a month in the summers, but it tapers down this time of year. I just adore weddings. Such a lovely celebration."

"Yes, it is, isn't it?" Stratton said, eyeing Emma over his cupcake. They ate the cupcake in silence. Clara, standing in front of them, wide-eyed, wringing her hands on her apron.

"This is absolutely the best cupcake I've ever eaten," Stratton said. "I taste a hint of, what? Lemon?"

"Yes. You don't think it's too much, do you?"

"No, not at all."

"Clara. These are beyond good. I love the lemon. It's not too much at all," Emma agreed.

"Good. All right then. Off I go," Clara said and left the dining room with the other cupcake, smiling.

Emma picked up her cell from the table. "Excuse me, I need to make a call," she said to Stratton.

"Of course, you do."

She sighed at him, hit a number on her keypad and waited.

"Hey, Joey. How are you this lovely Tuesday morning?"

"Hey, Emma. What's up? Don't tell me, let me guess. You're kayaking in Chillicothe."

"No wonder you're the top detective. You're psychic."

"And I got a call from Sheriff Lyla Day."

"Ahhh, yes. Lyla. So, you two dated? "

Joey laughed. "Dated? I guess you could call it that. Anyway, that's in the past and I don't look back."

"At the trail of broken hearts."

"Not with Day. She actually broke it off with me to marry her husband. Win some. Lose some. She's a sharp lady and a good cop."

"Would you have married her?"

"Let's talk about something else."

"Okay."

"Like, what are you doing down there nosing around and leaving poor Merek to do all your work up here? You're making this a habit. Poor Merek."

"Yes, poor, poor Merek."

"I ran into him at the Wildflower Cafe Saturday night with his girlfriend."

"Which one?"

Joey laughed.

"The tall blonde with legs up to her nose piercings."

"Which blonde?"

"That's for sure." He chuckled. "But I've seen him with this one quite a bit lately. They're always holding hands and necking, talking romantic mush in Polish, I guess. Disgusting."

"Ah, yes. Disgusting. I'm sure you've never done anything like that."

"You got me there. I've never spoken a word of Polish in my life. Look, I knew it would only be a matter of time after Day called before I heard from you. So what do you need?"

"You sound like I only call you when I want something."

"And?"

"Okay. You're right. But I did take you to dinner a few weeks ago at the Wildflower."

"Ahhh, yes. The best fried chicken around. I've eaten there the last three Saturday nights. Tasty. As I recall, it was your saying thank you for my getting the state police to help you clean up that mess in West Virginia. So, what's up this time?"

They talked about the shooting and she told him about the hair she took from the tree branch.

"If I send it up, how long to get the DNA report?"

"Couple weeks, at the earliest. It ain't CSI here, you know."

"Yeah. I know. Okay if I overnight it to you today?"

"Sure thing. I'll get it to the lab as soon as I get it. You, obviously, haven't shared this with Day, have you?"

She paused. "Not yet. And don't tell, okay? I just want to check it out and not waste her time if it turns out to be nothing. And we both know you can get it done quicker because you're the greatest detective on the face of the planet."

"Yeah, I know *that*. Okay. No problem. You've helped me out enough over the years. Hey, I wasn't going to tell you this, but I think I will. Merek put my and my date's fried chicken dinners on his expense account last weekend."

"So you've technically gotten paid twice for West Virginia and now you owe me."

They laughed.

"Send it Fed-X and I'll have my secretary bring it to me when it comes in."

"Thanks, Joey. Oh, and one more thing. Can you email me a list of all the registered kayaks in Ross County? I forgot to ask Merek."

"No problem."

"Great, thanks, Joey. Bye."

Stratton eyed her as she laid her cell on the table. "Emma, you're withholding evidence."

She scrunched up her face and shrugged. "You've never done it as a reporter, I'm sure."

"Well, alright. You've got me there. But that aside, you're withholding information from me. You never answered my question about going to Europe."

"Let's go paddle around Ross Lake. I need to think." She stood, putting her cell back in her purse.

Stratton stood, gave her a reluctant frown and sighed. "Alright. Let's go paddle Ross Lake so you can think."

Stratton and Emma paddled through the cypress tree knees along the east bank of Ross Lake. Two mallards swam in front of them, heads slightly swinging back and forth to keep an eye on the paddlers behind them, quacking softly to each other as if murmuring in deep conversation. *More than likely discussing the two*

*humans in the big plastic boats and wondering if they have any food,* Emma thought.

"What a lovely little lake." Stratton said as he paddled beside her.

Emma's stomach did that little butterfly-flip it'd been doing ever since she'd laid eyes on him three months ago when he was standing behind his desk at the *Stonefalls Post.* And she didn't like it. She didn't like it one bit. She didn't want to fall in love. Attraction, sex, romance, heartbreak; the four-step program she'd experienced once before and swore she'd never do it again. And she'd been successful for many years. Until now.

She'd dated several men, but it was nothing that ever became more than a few months of dinner dates, maybe some biking and kayaking now and then before she'd politely bow out for various created reasons, mainly, because she'd never really been that interested in anyone since the man who had broken her heart. Until now.

She smiled at him. She couldn't help herself. Stratton was the most dashing man she'd ever met. He was fit, trim, had a full head of thick silver-gray hair, was successful in business, and solid in his personal life. He had no baggage, no mess, and he was an expert lover. All signs of "Portage Ahead," as far as her head told her. But her heart told her to stay in her boat and keep paddling.

"I like it here," she said, watching a squirrel jump from a dead log and scramble up a tree.

"How did you become so interested in kayaking?" he asked.

"A friend turned me on to it, over ten years ago. She called me to cheer me up after my dad's funeral and asked if I wanted to go and I said yes. Next thing I know, I'm as hooked as a duck on the water. I just can't get enough of it. I love being outside; breathing the air, hearing the water drip off the paddle blade, watching the bow of my boat slice through the water. I like feeling my arms pump, helping me pick up speed. It's just so calming and exhilarating—all at the same time, no matter if I'm on a river or a lake. I've never felt anything like it. What about you?"

"Ann and I went rafting and then we took the kids on a rafting trip in West Virginia on a section of the New. It was flat water, beautiful scenery. It was a long time ago. Glen was ten and Ellen was twelve, so that was over thirty years ago." He laughed and paddled around a stump sticking above the water.

"You and Ann had Ellen when you were twenty years old? You and Ann were both in college. My. My. Was she an oops, Mr. Reeves?"

"No, not at all. We wanted to marry and start a family as soon as we were out of high school. We'd planned it since we'd started playing footsie in kindergarten."

Emma thought about that as she paddled. They'd been together for nearly all their lives. She couldn't imagine how devastated he must've felt when she died.

She had never come close to marriage or children in her life. It was something she never really thought about. She'd always been obsessed with work. Work and more work. Kayaking was about the only thing that she enjoyed more than work. Until now.

She'd answered an ad in the paper for a claims adjuster at Matrix when she was nineteen years old and loved it. She'd moved from Chillicothe, where she'd lived much of her life, but easily settled into Clintonville.

Helping people put their lives back together after a catastrophe made her feel good. She went on to get claims adjuster certifications and worked her way into the Special Investigative Unit, also called the SIU. There, she enjoyed working with several of the top investigators in the industry and the many police and law enforcement departments all over the country to help bring down people committing claims fraud and other crimes. That's where she met Joey Reed and they'd hit it off from the first case they'd worked on together.

"Does it bother you at all that I'm the same age as Ellen and older than Glen?"

"Not at all. Does it bother you that I'm old enough to be your father?"

Emma laughed. "No. Does it bother Ellen and Glen?"

"No, Emma. It doesn't. They're glad that I'm happy. It doesn't make me love them or their mother any less, but Ann's been gone for nearly six years. And she wanted me to remarry. We talked about it."

"Really?"

"Yes. She was kind, loving, and painfully realistic at those times when she needed to be. She was a strong woman."

They paddled lazily around the lake.

"She was an incredible artist, that's for sure. Those paintings in your office of you and Maggie fishing look almost like photographs. I still can't get over them."

"Several people offer to buy those paintings from me every year. There's no way I could sell any of them. They're the only ones I kept after she died. I gave the rest to the kids and her family."

"Is Rhonda watching Maggie at her house?"

"No, she's keeping the dog with her at my place. Gives her and the husband a little break from one another."

"Ahhhh....yes. I can imagine living with someone like Rhonda could be a bit tiring."

"And vice-versa. He's just as much of a character as she is."

She smiled. "Sometimes, likes attract."

"And sometimes not."

A hoot owl called from across the lake. They sat bobbing on the water for several minutes. The sky grew purple, red, and orange and the sun slid down and disappeared over the horizon. The air grew cooler.

"What a beautiful sunset. You know, sometimes the most beautiful things in life *are* free. We just don't see them because we're too busy trying to buy our happiness," she said.

"Wise words, my dear."

"Let's head back and load up."

"Sounds good."

They paddled to the bank beside the parking lot, put the kayaks in the bed of Stratton's truck, and secured their gear inside the boats before they climbed in and shut the doors.

They pulled out of the parking lot and onto Hydell Road, not noticing Jebediah Pierce watching them while he sat in his car with his fishing poles sticking up in the backseat.

# CHAPTER 9

"Whatever you do, mother, don't go off the rails. This man is obviously wanting something."

"Why shouldn't I be upset? Your father is stalking me and shows up after fifty-seven years and you expect me to be calm. Am I supposed to offer him tea and cakes and chat sweetly with him?"

"I understand. It's simply unacceptable that he's been following you. But we must remain calm. I've already hired more security guards to watch the house."

"I'll have him arrested and thrown in prison where he belongs if he messes with me." She paced the large living room. "I most certainly will." She hit the back of the leather couch with her fist.

"Oh, mother. Don't be ridiculous. You're simply talking nonsense. Calm yourself." He held his chin and walked around the room. Not surprisingly, the room had a historical golfing theme throughout. Old wooden clubs hung on the walls, along with expensive prints of golf courses all over the world on their opening days. Mary had played in tournaments at all of them—and usually won.

"Well—" she was interrupted as the doorbell chimed through the house. They stared at one another as Mary's butler, John, answered the door.

Seconds later, he walked into the room with a puzzled look on his face. "A Mr. Wellington to see you both" he said, with a questioning tone.

"Thank you, John. Show him in," she said, standing tall in her designer suit, cut to perfection and highlighting her curves. At seventy-six, Mary was one good-looking woman.

John nodded and walked back into the foyer. A weary looking, thin man in a polyester brown suit crept into the room like a frightened animal. He stood with a brimmed wool hat in his shaking hands and looked at Mary then at Charles. Mary put a hand to her throat and her eyes grew wide.

"You're my son? Charles Wellington the third?"

Charles was stunned. He didn't answer and turned away. *Polyester? How could I be related at all to this man?*

"Mary, it's good to see you. You look much more beautiful than you do on television."

"So you said in your note. What do you want?"

"May I sit down?"

"Most certainly not."

"What is it you want?" Charles leaned on the stone fireplace that had been rebuilt about two years ago. He'd given Mary many of the stones in it from rivers he and Emma had kayaked together over the past sixteen years.

"I'm sorry about the note. One too many drinks, I guess. I was going to approach you, but—"

"But what? You'd rather stalk me and send me a note like a ten-year-old child? You always were irresponsible. I guess aging didn't help you mature."

"Please, Mary. Can't we be civil?"

"Say what you've come to say and then leave the premises and don't return," Charles said.

The man stared at him with a smile. "What a fine man you grew into."

"Why are you here?" Mary demanded.

The man straightened, raised his head then looked back down at the Persian rug. "I'm here to let Charles know the truth."

"What was that?" she snipped.

The man raised his head and glared at Mary. "It's time to tell Charles why I *really* wasn't in his life."

Mary burst into laughter.

"I'm well aware that you walked out on mother days after I was born," Charles said.

The frail man turned from Charles and stared at Mary.

Mary laughed again. "What so-called *truth* are you going to tell him?"

"The truth about why I wasn't here for him," the man said meekly.

Charles glanced at Mary then turned back to look at this stranger who'd come into his life. He really couldn't see a single feature they shared; his nose, his eyes, his mouth? And certainly not the way he dressed or his demeanor. It didn't really matter. He was growing agitated by this man who looked like a vagabond.

"Mr. Wellington, we don't want you here or near us again. If you refuse to leave the area, we'll have a restraining order drawn against you and have you arrested if you're seen near either my mother or me. She will have undercover security with her at all times."

The man raised his eyes to Charles's. He turned and began to walk toward the door. He put his hat on his head and turned back around to face them.

"I understand. But I want him to know the truth," he said to Mary, nodding toward Charles.

"Get out and don't you *ever* come back here," she screamed, her red fingernails digging into the back of the couch.

It was nearly six-thirty when Charles sat with his mother at the small table in her glassed-in porch. The fading sun was sinking behind the rise of the fifth green.

She sipped a martini and Charles tapped the glass of his Crown Ambassador Reserve with his right fingers. A beau of Mary's in Australia had the beer shipped to her several times a year.

"Do you think he's gone?" Charles asked.

"How should I know?" Mary replied quickly, taking another sip of her drink. She put a tanned hand on Charles's arm. "Oh, sweetheart, I'm sorry. I'm just so upset. This is all simply nonsense."

"Mother, we shouldn't let this man get to us. He's a stranger, no less than a hoodlum, and perhaps a crook, waltzing in here. And what is this 'truth' he was talking about?"

"It's nothing we need to discuss. It's my reputation, Charles. I don't want him damaging it."

Charles laughed and took another drink of his beer.

"What's that supposed to mean?"

"Mother, I think you've done a thorough job of damaging your own reputation. You were just in the tabloids again this week. It's always joyous to see a picture of my mother plastered on the front of *Raging Celebrities Magazine Sports Edition* lying on my secretary's desk. It disturbs me that Kathy reads such trash."

"That's not damaging. That's PR. There's a difference."

Mary's iPhone buzzed on the table. She reached for it, her bright red fingernails clicked on the face of it. She put the phone to her ear and smiled. "Devereux, darling. How lovely of you to call. Are you still taking the red-eye in for breakfast and a game in the morning? Yes. I'll have my limo pick you up. Oh, of course, dear." She laughed.

Mary was a popular woman, especially with the men. The cover of the latest tabloid he'd seen lying on Kathy's desk, noted that Mary was currently involved with a foreign movie director whom she'd met while golfing in the south of France, who was married and, blahblahblah, and who was probably on the phone with her right now. Charles really didn't care. He'd grown weary of Mary's escapades over the years.

He got up and walked into the library. He loved this room. He moved slowly around it and glanced at the books on the shelves. When he was a child, his mother would buy him dozens of books. He'd sit at the mahogany desk, working mathematic problems, feeling the thrill of success after solving problem after problem, Samuel praising him and pushing him to do more. He often thought of his tutor. He needed to look him up sometime.

He glanced down at the desk and saw the same tabloid that he'd seen on Kathy's desk. *Oh, Mother.* He'd bet she collected all of them.

John, Mary's butler, walked into the room with a feather duster. He always looked elegant in a black velvet vest, black pants, and a starched white shirt. He was in his late sixties and his gray hair had thinned a great deal since Charles had first met him. He'd been Mary's butler for nearly a decade.

"Charles, how good to see you."

"You too, John. How've you been?"

"Fine. Fine. Your mother has given me the weekend off and I'm going to Hocking Hills with the wife, staying in your mother's chalet. She doesn't seem to use it much and told me I could stay there anytime. The leaves are beautiful this time of year, so I decided to take her up on the offer."

"Yes this is a beautiful time of year. The leaves are vibrant. I enjoyed them while kayaking Saturday on Paint Creek. You say she doesn't use the chalet much? Why doesn't she just sell it?"

John began dusting a bookcase and chuckled. "You know your mother."

107

"Yes. That I do. The collector of everything–namely men."

He stopped dusting and turned to Charles. "I don't pry into Mrs. Wellington's affairs–of any kind, but I couldn't help but overhearing the conversation. Was that Mr. Wellington really your father?"

Charles nodded slowly. "So it seems."

"I see. Well, do you and Mary intend to do anything further about *him*?"

"I was going to speak with you about it. We've informed security, but could you also keep an eye out and if you see the man appear anywhere, call the authorities immediately and then call me. I'm also going to hire another body guard for her, without her knowing. She doesn't usually have any with her. She hates it. She'd be furious. But I'd appreciate it if you could assist me with this. Legally, he has no attachment to the estate or any of mother's money, if that's what he's after."

"I most certainly will. Is he dangerous?"

"Good question. He looks harmless. But I don't know. I don't know him at all. My mother, obviously, did fifty-eight years ago, but people certainly change over time."

"Well, I'm not so sure about that. I think we often just get taller and older." He went back to dusting and then stopped. "Come to think of it, I did see that man about two weeks ago. He was sitting in the park on a bench. It makes sense now. After I passed him, I could feel his eyes on me. Disturbing."

"Quite. Well, you know what to do. I need to be off. I just wanted to stay and have a drink with mother and make sure she'd calmed down after his visit. Seems she's fine. She's on the phone making plans for morning tee time."

"Ahhhh, yes, Devereux, the film director." He

rolled his eyes.

"Indeed. Well, I'd best be off. Thank you, John."

"Not a problem. Call me if you need anything and I'll certainly keep my eyes peeled."

"Thank you, John."

Charles walked down the long hallway into the kitchen. He placed his empty beer glass in the sink and left the house.

He started his Lexus and put it in reverse when his iPhone rang. He knew it would be Mary, not pleased with him having left without saying goodbye.

He shoved the gearshift back into park, pulled the phone from his inside jacket pocket without looking at the face of it, hit the talk icon with his thumb and put the phone to his right ear.

"Yes?" he said.

Silence.

"Hello? Mother?"

"Charles."

His heart stopped.

"It's me. Can you talk?"

# CHAPTER 10

Ron and Charles sat in a booth at the Wildflower Café eating breakfast and reading the Wednesday morning edition of *The Columbus Dispatch* on their iPads. Charles finished reading the paper and opened the latest issue of the community newspaper, *The Booster*, bringing himself up-to-date on the latest Clintonville news. He scanned through the headlines, shut off his iPad, and looked at Ron.

"I need to get to the office. I've got a teleconference with the Defense Department at ten," Charles said.

"Yes, that's right."

"You didn't touch your meal. Something wrong?" Ron asked, wiping his mouth with his napkin and swiping the check off the table.

"Just not hungry this morning. Look, I can pay for that," Charles said, reaching for the check.

"You paid last time."

"And your point?"

"It's my turn."

They walked to the register together, Ron limping slightly from the broken leg he'd received in a car accident while leaving Charles's house in July. Ron paid the bill and they walked outside and started toward their vehicles.

"Ron, I need to talk to you about something. Oh, never mind. I simply can't go into it right now."

"What's that?" Ron said, as he hit the remote to unlock his Acura sedan.

"Oh, nothing. Well, actually, I do need to speak with you about something. But I have to get to the office right now. I'll call you later."

"Sounds fine. Good luck with the teleconference."

"Thank you."

"Oh, Charles?"

Charles had one leg in his SUV and was starting to slide under the wheel. He stopped, stood, and looked over the roof at Ron. "Yes?"

"I have to work late tonight and I have a karate class tomorrow, but I can pop by Weiland's and pick up a bottle of wine, grab a pizza at Dante's, and come over after class tomorrow night. Would that work? We could talk then."

Charles looked at him for a long moment. "Actually, I can't. I have an appointment tomorrow evening."

Ron acted deflated, but quickly collected himself. He smiled. "Okay. Well, I'll just talk to you later then." He got into his car and drove out of the lot.

Charles sat in his SUV and watched Ron's car disappear down Indianola Avenue. He smacked the steering wheel. "Why didn't I just tell him?"

He sighed deeply as his left pinkie finger began to twitch.

Robert walked out of the dining room with the last of the breakfast dishes.

"Oh, no. Nooooh. Nooooo," Emma said in a sad tone, reading the front page of *The Chillicothe Gazette* lying in front of her on the table.

Stratton lowered *The New York Times* he was reading and peered over the top of it. "What in the world is wrong, Emma?"

"They've arrested Tammy Eastland for the

attempted murder of Alder Mycon."

"What?" Stratton sat taller in his chair.

"They found the rifle that fired the bullet hidden in her closet. That's about all it says, really. Just mentions that other facts remain confidential due to the investigation" She scanned the article again and looked at Stratton. "My, God, I've helped to hang the poor woman. It's just not right."

"Well, I guess that solves it," he said, snapping the paper and raising it in front of him.

"No, it doesn't solve *it*. She didn't do it. I know she didn't do it."

He lowered the paper again. "And how do you *know* that, honey? You don't know her at all – or the situation. You said the sheriff is bright and knows what she's doing. It looks like a pretty open and shut case, sorry to say, for Tammy."

"It's just not right. Something's very wrong."

"Like what?"

"It's too easy. Too... I don't know. Just doesn't feel right. I spent enough time with Tammy to know she wouldn't shoot anyone. She's too... Well, prissy for one thing. And neat and clean for another. And why would she do such a thing after all this time? She has a new life and she seems happy. And if she did do it, I don't think she'd be this blatantly stupid about it. She could've stuck her hair under a ball cap and not worn a coat she wears all the time, not driven her own car, and certainly not used her own gun and put it back in her closet. Come on. She's a bright woman."

"Many people *seem* to be what they are, but you and I both know, especially in our lines of work, they're often very different."

"I know. I know. But I'm right this time and I'm going to prove it. I'll be right back. I need to call Joey."

He gave her a long look before he snapped his

paper back open and continued reading.

Several minutes later she returned, laid her cell on the table, and plopped in her chair. She crossed her arms in front of her like a pouting child and looked toward Stratton, still hidden behind his paper.

"Joey doesn't have the DNA back yet from the hair. I can't believe we can put a man on the moon, but can't get DNA back quicker than we do. I called the sheriff, too. Tammy's been released on bail and I'm going to see if she'll talk to me today. And Alder's sister, Willow, may call me for lunch so you'll have to find something to do on your own. That is, if I can get her to go. I'm sorry."

Stratton lowered the paper and glared at her.

"What?"

"I was hoping we could book our trip for Europe online this afternoon and get the quickest flight out. Especially now, since this is over."

"Look, I'm just not ready to go to Europe right now. I need to stick around here. I'm working this case. It's not over."

Stratton folded the paper, laid it on the table, stood, and walked around behind her chair. He bent over and started kissing her neck as he wrapped his arms around her from behind. "I want to kiss you in London and make love to you in Rome. And I've been thinking..."

Her cell rang.

He huffed and stepped away.

"Stratton, I... I... Oh, I..." She reached for him, glanced at the ringing phone, then back at him.

"Are you going to get that?" he said, pointing at the phone.

"I'm sorry, yes. I really should." She grabbed the phone, stood, and strolled across the room away from him as she checked the number. It said, "Unknown." She felt a flash of anger. *Simon Johnson, the bastard, is calling me again?*

Stratton walked back to his chair and sat down. He squeezed the bridge of his nose.

"*Hello?*" Emma said roughly into the phone.

"Oh. Yes," she said with a much softer voice. "Alder, hi. How are you? Well, that's great. Sure. No problem. I can be there in about twenty minutes. Yes. Okay. Fine. No. Not a problem at all. Good-bye." She ended the call and walked back to the table where Stratton was sitting, watching her, hands folded in front of him on the table.

"That was Alder Mycon. He asked if I could pick him up at the hospital right now and take him home. He wants to talk to me about Tammy's arrest."

Stratton stared at her.

"Stratton, I'm sorry. But could we just put the Europe discussion on hold until we can both talk about it later?"

He looked down at his hands. He took a deep breath and let it out slowly.

"Please?" She walked behind him and put her arms around him and kissed the top his head. "Come with me to pick up Alder?" she asked.

He stood and walked past her and up the stairs to the bedrooms, without looking her way. A door closed a few seconds later.

She stared up the stairway. "I don't *need* this. I do not *need* this," she said under her breath.

She stomped out the back door and slammed it behind her, jumped in her truck, tossed her cell on the dash, and shifted into drive. The tires chirped as she pulled out of the lot. As soon as she was on the road, she floored the gas pedal. The bed of the truck fishtailed and the smell of rubber seeped into the cab.

"Why did he do *that*? If this is love, forget it!" she yelled.

She slowed down and pulled into an empty church parking lot and stared out the windshield for several seconds at a small graveyard. She picked up the cell from the dash and started to call him, but stopped. Instead she made another call. Charles answered on the third ring.

"Hello, Emma. How are you?"

"I'll tell you how I am. Fed up. Fed, totally, up — with men and romance and all the guilt trips and everything that goes along with it. That's how I am. Exactly how I am."

"I see. So you and the handsome Stratton Reeves have had your first tiff, I'm suspecting?"

"You bet we did."

"About my calling you in the middle of your *nap*?"

"No. He asked me to go to Europe with him. He wants to make reservations and leave right now."

Silence.

"Charles?"

"I fail to see why you're upset."

"I can't go to Europe. I need to crack this case. Can you believe him? He's a reporter. He should know better. He should understand."

"Emma, he's in love with you. Are you that surprised that he wants to whisk you off to beautiful places?"

"Well, yes. No. Maybe. I don't really know. All I know is he ruined everything. He shouldn't have asked. Oh, why did I have to meet him anyway? I wish I'd never laid eyes on the man."

"Stop it. Stop it this instant! I want you to just stop talking and listen to me, Emma Haines. Stratton Reeves is a good man. In fact, I believe he's the perfect man for you. And you know you care about him deeply. I believe you *are* in love with him, as well. But you're still afraid and too stubborn to admit it. So what, you got your

115

heart broken once. It happens to all of us, so just get over it. Move on, and stop acting so immature about it. This is all part of being in a relationship, Emma."

Charles took a deep breath, then continued. "Now, I want you to just take some deep breaths and calm down. Right this second. Do it. I want to hear you breathing, not talking or wailing or yelling. Do it. Come on. Do it. Breathe."

She closed her eyes and took two deep breaths. "This speech sounds familiar. You still mad at me?"

"No. Not now. Although I did think about flipping you in your kayak Saturday, but I'm not mad at you anymore. Now, let's talk this through."

"I'd love to, but I can't right now. I'm on my way to pick up Alder at the hospital. They arrested Tammy, his ex-wife, and he wants to talk to me about it. And I've got a tentative lunch appointment with Willow Mycon, Alder's sister, and I want to try to talk to Tammy too. I'll call you back later and bring you up to speed. Okay?"

"Fine. But you will only call me back after you've thought about this like a mature, intelligent woman. Correct?"

"Yes, Daddy. I will. Good-bye."

"Be careful, Emma."

She ended the call and started to call Stratton's cell again, but stopped. "I just can't talk to him right now."

She tossed the phone in the console and drove to the hospital.

After making small talk for thirty minutes with Alder Mycon in her truck, Emma pulled onto his farm's gravel lane that led up the side of a fence row. Four horses grazed lazily in the field and cows walked along the ridge behind a gigantic, old brick farmhouse. "Place looks like it's out of *Southern Living Magazine*," she said.

"Thanks. I like it. It's all mine and I'm proud of it. Been in the family since the Civil War and I intend to keep it up as long as I can."

"What kind of horses are those? Paints?"

"Yes. Only kind of horse I buy. They can be somewhat temperamental, but they're fun to ride. You ride?"

She shook her head, "I'll stick to riding rivers in my kayak."

They parked in front of the house and got out of the truck. Alder walked onto the porch and unlocked a side door. Emma followed him through a large mud room and into a kitchen the size of her condo, complete with skylight, stainless steel appliances, and tiled flooring.

"Wow. This is amazing."

"Thanks. Go ahead and have a seat at the table. Tammy picked everything out, had the Amish make all the cabinets, table, chairs and all the wood trim, but I installed it all myself. Can I get you anything to drink? Tea, juice, milk, a beer?"

"Just water, thanks," she said as she pulled out a rounded spindle-back chair and sat down at a table large enough to feed sixteen people.

"Sure." He reached in a cupboard, pulled out a glass, filled it halfway with crushed ice and topped it off with water from the dispensers on the front of the door.

"Think I'll have some tomato juice. Just sounds good." He pulled out a small can from the fridge, popped the top, and took a drink. He walked to the table and sat down opposite Emma.

"I want to talk to you about Tammy. She didn't shoot me. I know she didn't."

"And how do you know that? Everything is pointing right at her."

"I know, but it's not her. She'd never do that to me. Ever."

"You sound pretty sure of yourself. Want to tell me why?"

"Because Tammy and I never stopped caring about each other. We just couldn't live together. We had different priorities."

Emma looked around the kitchen. "Seems she left a nice home behind. Looks like she left everything behind."

"She did. She moved into an apartment when we split up, but we'd agreed on what she'd take when she got her own house. And then she remarried and didn't need anything, after all."

He took a long swig of juice. "Truth is, I wanted her to stay at home and she wanted a career. This place is big and I just wanted her to be a farmer's wife once I inherited it. But, she'd always dreamed of being *a career woman* so we parted. That's all."

After meeting Tammy, Emma could buy that. She couldn't picture Tammy as a "down-on-the-farm" girl. But she felt Alder wasn't telling her everything.

"If she loves you so much, why'd she marry Taylor Eastland six months after your divorce?"

Alder eyed her. "You've been doing your homework haven't you?" He smiled. He had the biggest dimples Emma had ever seen. She could picture the perfect Tammy and Alder, walking down the aisle in the perfect church, her long flowing perfect gown trailing behind her, Alder standing with his back to the altar, beaming at his perfect bride.

Stratton popped into her mind, the back of his head as he was walking up the steps at the bed and breakfast. She sighed and took a drink of her water. It tasted like her grandmother's water when she was a kid and Emma figured it was probably from a well.

"That's what I do; lots of research to track down the bad guys and learn about the good ones. Well, I used to. Now I train insurance investigators how to do it. But my experience does come in handy."

He nodded. "That's good."

"So, you never answered my question. If Tammy loved you so much, why the quick marriage?"

He shrugged. "Maybe he offered her the job of a lifetime and a big diamond ring. She said she needed to be married to someone who would let her work. Taylor sure does that. Don't get me wrong, he's a good man and all. I have no hard feelings, as long as he treats her right."

Emma looked around the kitchen and took another drink. "So why'd you call me anyway? Why not someone else? Why not Forrest or Willow?"

"You really need to ask *that*? You saw them. I really don't have anything to do with them. They're pretty much my siblings by blood, believe it or not, but we don't do anything together. Haven't for years."

"Until Saturday."

"Yeah, until then."

"So why *did* you go kayaking with him again?"

"Well, like I said before, Forrest said he needed to talk to me about something. Something that he couldn't talk about to anyone else and said he thought it'd be nice if we went kayaking. It'd be relaxing and a private place to talk."

"Did that strike you as odd? Why couldn't you just talk at his place or here or in a bar?"

"Well, yeah. Kind of. But I don't know him, really. And he said it would be like when we were kids and dad would take us down the Paint."

"So what'd he want to tell you?"

119

"I don't know. We mostly talked about the creek and kayaking and then I got shot. I still can't believe it." He took a drink of juice. "And I still can't believe Tammy's in jail for it. You have to help her, Ms. Haines. She didn't do it. That's why I called you. You need to find out who shot me."

"Why me? Why don't you call the sheriff to help you?"

"They're the ones that arrested her. They already think she did it. But she didn't. I just know it. She has no reason to. I just can't figure it all out. And you're some kind of an investigator. I don't know any other investigators." He shook his head like a sad puppy.

"Well, I'm... Anyway, look. Let me ask you this. Are you dating anyone that she may know about and be jealous?"

He shook his head again. "I haven't dated since we divorced. I don't have time. And no desire either. I miss her. And I didn't cheat on her either. I have no idea where Willow gets her information, but that's a flat-out lie and Tammy will tell you it is too."

"You still in love with her?"

"Of course I am. I can't help it. If you ever met her you'd know why. She's the most beautiful, kind woman you'd ever want to meet. Smart too."

She had to agree with him, even with the little she knew about her. He didn't need to know she'd met Tammy.

"Alder, how'd you swing a day off during harvest season to go kayaking?"

"Well, I have help. I mean, I can't keep this place up all alone. I have five local guys that help me out. They brought a couple of their cousins to help Saturday. I hated doing it because it costs me more money, but Forrest sounded so..."

"So what?"

"Desperate. When he called me last week, he just sounded so desperate."

"When did he call you and exactly what did he say?"

"He called me the Sunday before we went kayaking. It was late, Sunday night. He said he'd like to get together and talk to me about something that was really bugging him and he could only talk to me about it. I kept asking him what it was about, but he wouldn't say. Said he had to tell me in person, somewhere quiet and peaceful, then he said, 'Hey, we haven't been on Paint Creek since we was kids, so I got us two kayaks and we can paddle and talk." He mimicked Forrest.

"And you didn't think that was strange at all?"

"Look, the last time I even saw Forrest was two years ago at Dad's funeral. We don't go to the same places, even though it is a small town. That's the first I'd heard from him since then, and before that, I didn't talk to him at all, for years. Hadn't seen or heard from either him or Willow since they moved out, really. Me and Tammy got married in college, dad got sick, and we came back home to run the farm, then dad died. Except, Tammy didn't care for the farm life–at all."

"How much of this place did Forrest and Willow inherit?"

"None. Dad wrote them out of the will. He didn't leave them a dime. Nothing. He knew they were worthless. They started going down that path in junior high school. Neither of them wanted to do anything but chase the opposite sex and drink. Later on, they just wanted to get high all the time."

"How'd they feel about you inheriting everything?"

"Not good. They said it was unfair, but they also never helped Dad do a thing around here, even when they lived here. And, as you can tell, they're not the sharpest sticks in the pile either. I can't believe I'm related to them, honestly. But, I am. At least that's what

121

I've always been told and I grew up with them. We were all here, in this house."

Emma laughed. "You three are very different. Hey, while I'm thinking about it, you wouldn't happen to know a guy in town named Jebediah Pierce would you?"

He thought about it, shook his head. "No, can't say that I do. Why?"

"No reason. Just wondered."

They sat in silence for a few seconds.

"So, will you help me find out who really shot me?" Alder asked.

Emma started to answer him when her cell rang. She dug it out of her purse.

"Hello," she said, still looking at Alder.

"Oh, hi. Yes, sure. I'd love to meet you for lunch, Willow. Noon? Okay, where? Yes, I do know where Jerry's Pizza on Paint Street is. Fine. See you in about an hour."

"You're meeting my sister for lunch?"

Emma looked at him as she slipped the phone back in her purse.

"You don't think Tammy shot me, either, do you?"

"Can't say one way or the other right now. I need more information and I'm hoping your sister will help me out."

"No idea what *she'll* be able to tell you. Yesterday in the hospital was the first time I'd seen her in years." He shook his head and finished off his tomato juice.

"Well, I intend to find out," she said.

# CHAPTER 11

Charles walked into his office and closed the door. He sat down and stared at his desk for several minutes. There was a slight tap on his door before his secretary, Kathy, peeked in. He pulled himself together and smiled.

"Good morning, Charles."

"Oh, good morning, Kathy. I'm glad you're here. I need an update on Constable. I have a conference call in two hours."

"Sure thing. I'll bring it up and we can run through it."

Kathy walked over to the small conference table, sat down, and hit a few buttons. A keyboard flipped up in front of her, a screen dropped down from the ceiling, and within seconds, Kathy had the project report showing on the screen.

Charles got up from his desk and sat down beside her.

"Take me to the last time we checked its orbit."

A few clicks and slide fourteen appeared.

"Any problems?"

"None reported. Everyone has updated the file as of last night at ten."

Charles stared at the screen. Something wasn't right. Something was off, but he couldn't put his finger on it.

"Go back to slide twelve, please."

Slide twelve appeared on the screen. "The orbit is one-tenth of a degree wider than last month. Is there an explanation?"

Kathy brought up a different file of notes.

"Appears to be a slight temperature change in the satellite's skin, that's what Gary reported three days ago."

"I don't recall anyone mentioning this. I need an explanation immediately."

"Certainly." She typed on the keyboard. "Is there anything else?"

"No, that's all. Thank you, Kathy."

"I'll contact Gary."

"Thank you."

Kathy shut down the system and stood, the screen climbed silently back into the ceiling behind her as she faced him.

"How was your kayak trip?"

"A catastrophe."

"What? Not again."

"Yes. Again. And, well...I can't go into it right now."

"How's Ron? I miss him around here."

Charles looked away from her toward his Macintosh monitor as he answered. "He's fine. We had breakfast together. He said to send you and the twins his love." He pretended to be reading. "That'll be all for now. Please close my door as you leave." He gave her a quick smile and tapped his mouse.

"Sure thing." Kathy left his office and gently closed the door behind her.

He took a deep breath, dropped his head in his hands, and ran his fingers through his hair. He was having a difficult time concentrating on work. Simon would be at his house tomorrow evening at eight and his stomach was in knots. He hadn't slept or eaten since he'd received Simon's call while he was leaving Mary's the night before.

"Maybe Emma's right about relationships," he said aloud.

He opened his jacket, slid out his iPhone, and tapped the screen. He got Emma's voice mail, but didn't leave a message.

He laid the phone on his desk and studied it. Finally, he turned his leather chair around to his Mac again and glanced through his emails, became frustrated, and began surfing the Internet for dinner ideas.

He loved to cook and now he'd be cooking for Simon tomorrow night, after nearly three years. Twenty minutes later, he'd decided to make the same meal he'd made the night Simon walked out on him. It had been Simon's favorite; pork loin stuffed with cherries boiled in port wine, shredded carrots, and shaved asparagus.

As he smiled at his decision, Kathy tapped on his door. "Charles, Gary is on line two. He believes there may be a serious problem with Constable."

The red light on Charles's phone blinked. Kathy raised both her eyebrows at him before she gently closed the door. He punched the light and picked up the receiver.

"Gary, report, please."

"Constable is pulling out of orbit."

"Yes, I saw that on the report. Minute, but definitely a concern that I trust will be corrected at once. Why didn't you mention this in the update meeting?"

"Because I felt it was something minor and I could adjust the calibration."

"And?"

"It's not possible. The satellite will hit Earth in twelve days."

Charles stared at his iPhone that was vibrating on his desk.

"Please get the team together and meet in the lab immediately ."

"Yes, sir."

He grabbed his cell too late to catch the call. He

checked his missed calls and the number didn't register. He couldn't even hit redial. "Damn it!"

He stood and paced the room, stopping in front of the whiteboard which contained high level notes of Constable. No detailed notes were written on executive whiteboards, only in secured lab areas. Charles crossed his arms and read through them several times. Something was sitting inside his head, at the base of his skull, tickling like a small itch. He looked at the notes again.

He walked to his desk and brought up the detailed files of the project on his computer and started reading the last report, going back in time. On the fifth post-launch report, he began jotting notes on the legal pad in front of him until he dialed in to his conference call.

The call with the Defense Department went well. It was for another project bid and they insisted on talking to Charles before they would sign the contract for several billion. They did both. Another feather in Charles's engineering hat.

Now, Charles sat with Gary and his team in the lab looking at the whiteboard as Charles drew a circle around a calculation.

"If we multiply this by its square root, it will adjust the temperature and keep Constable in orbit. That's my theory. Gary?"

"Yes. It could work."

"You'll let me know your findings in four hours, here in this lab, with the team. Now, you'll have to excuse me, ladies and gentlemen," Charles said, walking toward the door without waiting for a reply.

He closed the door to his office and his phone vibrated. His heart jolted.

"Emma, where are you?"

"Whoa. Don't snap at me. You called me, Grumpy."

"I'm not grumpy. I'm simply juggling."

"How many pins are in the air now?"

"Three large ones, to be exact. What's going on with you?"

Emma brought him up to speed on the case. "So what do you think?"

"I *think* you need to be careful. If this Jeb character was talking to that horrible creature, Forrest, he's certainly up to no good either."

"I will."

"How are you and Stratton getting along?"

Emma didn't answer.

"Are you still there?"

"Charles, I need to talk to you. I mean really *talk* to you."

Charles sat straighter in his chair. *Does she know about Simon?*

"What is it?"

"I think I'm falling in love and I don't want to."

Charles sat back in his chair and laughed. It was the first real laugh he'd had in months. "Why, Emma Haines. Love is nonexclusive, my dear. It happens to the best of us. Even you. As a matter of fact, I need to talk to you too."

"Really, what... Hey, Merek's trying to call and I really need to talk to him. I'll call you back later."

The iPhone went silent in Charles's hand and he put it down on his desk. He was still chuckling as he drummed his fingers and stared at the Constable report on the monitor.

He stopped laughing and stared at the screen.

He had to be right.

There was simply no room for error.

While he recalculated his equation for the ninth time, his iPhone chimed. He jumped.

"Hello, mother."

"I met with your father again. Everything's been taken care of. He's going back to the rock he crawled out from under in California. We won't hear from him again."

"What do you mean?" Charles asked. He checked his Vacheron-Constantin watch which his mother had bought for him in London the last time she'd played golf there. He had to meet Gary and the team in less than ten minutes in the lab. He leaned back in his leather office chair and propped his feet on his desk. He made a mental note to have Kathy get his shoes shined.

"My head of security handed him a restraining order and escorted him to the airport with a one-way ticket."

Charles slid his legs from his desk and stood. "You did what?"

"He hitchhiked out here and I wanted him as far away as quickly as possible. I would've asked you to build a rocket to strap him into, but there's not time for that. He got on the plane. He's gone."

"He returned to California?"

"Yes. Outside L.A. in a little town called St. Hills."

"Yes, I know. Emma had Merek conduct a background check on him," Charles said, walking toward the glass wall in his office that overlooked the Olentangy River.

"And what did he find out?"

He filled her in. "My grandparents are deceased and my father rents a room in a boarding house. He owns nothing, lives on his monthly social security check, can't find employment, and volunteers at a cancer hospital."

"How sweet," Mary said dryly.

"What's all this about, mother? This, 'Telling me the

truth' he babbled about."

Mary said nothing for several seconds. "I don't care for your tone, Charles."

He took a deep breath, but said nothing.

"Anyway, I bought him a ticket home. Oh, honey, I'm sorry about all this. Look, I have to run. Love to Ron, Emma, and the boys. Don't worry about your father. He won't be back. Toodles."

Charles slid his iPhone into his inside suit pocket and stood staring out the window at the slow-moving Olentangy river. It looked like a giant gray snake slithering past him, joining the Scioto downstream. He felt a sudden urge to be in his kayak, alone on a river, far away from where he stood.

A large black turkey buzzard flew close to the window and Charles watched it, gliding in large circles, high into the sky and back down again.

Emma slid into a booth at Jerry's Pizza and watched the door for Willow. The smell of pizza floated through the air and her mouth watered. A waitress walked over and greeted her with a huge smile and asked if she'd like something to drink. Emma asked for a glass of water and told her she was waiting on someone. The woman left and returned with her water. *Great pizza and friendly service,* Emma thought, taking a sip of her water.

Jerry's Pizza on Paint Street was an icon throughout the region. Pizzas had been made across from the Mead Paper Mill, now Gladfelter, since 1954. Emma loved the tasty squares and always wondered about the secret recipe that made it the one-of-a-kind pizza people craved.

It was the kind of place where everyone in town, from mill workers to white collar executives, converged for great pizza and a cold beer, especially on the weekends, just to relax and swap life stories.

She loved Jerry's pizza. It was a rare treat and she'd gotten Charles and Merek hooked on them too. She had to remember to pick up a couple of pies for Merek before she left town. She'd frequented Jerry's often when she'd lived in Chillicothe.

Her favorite pizza back home in Clintonville was Dante's. It had been in Clintonville for 40 years, a great family-owned and operated place and it was just a few blocks from her condo, in the same shopping plaza where Weiland's Market was located. She enjoyed pizzas from there often. The first meal she and Charles had ever shared was a Dante's pizza, about sixteen years ago.

After twenty minutes of listening to her stomach growl and thinking about her argument with Stratton, she thought Willow had stood her up until she came bursting through the door.

Emma suppressed her amazement at Willow's bright yellow outfit; a huge t-shirt, with the words "Dynamite Diva" written in sequins on the front, hung over a ratty pair of sweat pants. She carried a green jacket on her left arm, covering half of a torn red plastic tote.

Emma stood as Willow approached. "Hi, Willow. Glad you could make it."

She gave Emma a disgusted look as she pushed the table toward Emma's side of the booth and heaved herself in. By the time she got settled, she was sweating and huffing as if she'd climbed a mountain.

"It ain't easy getting someone to watch them kids, so I had to leave them with the oldest. I don't want to stay too long. I almost didn't come. Like I said, I don't have nothing to say to you. I already thanked you for helping Alder."

"I'll bet it is tough being a single mom," Emma replied.

"You got kids?"

"No. I never thought I was fit for the job."

Willow frowned at her. "What's that mean?"

"It means, Willow, that I just never wanted children," she said, growing more impatient with Ms. Mycon by the second. She took a deep breath and tried to soften her voice. "I have a dog, though. A basset named Murray. He's my kid. Your dog's really cute. She looks like she's going to have puppies any second."

"Damn dog is just something else that drives me crazy. Kids wanted a dog and no one pays any attention to it."

"Would you like to get rid of her?"

Willow eyed her. "Why, you interested? I'll sell her to you."

"How much?"

She shrugged. "I don't know. A hundred bucks." She laughed.

Emma pulled her checkbook out of her purse. "Sure thing. I'll write you a check. When can I pick her up?"

Willow's eyes flew open wide. "You mean you're going to buy that mutt for a hundred bucks?"

"Yes. When can I get her?"

Emma ripped the check off and handed it to her. Willow grabbed it and gave her a puzzled look. "You know, I'm not sure who you are, but I don't think I want to talk to you no more."

"Look, I know you don't have to talk to me, but I just want to find out who shot your brother. Don't you want to know?"

"I done told you, I already know. It was Tammy. Tammy Eastland. That's who shot him. You seen her run through the woods, didn't ya?"

"What do you mean?" Emma asked.

Willow's eyes fluttered before she looked away.

"I really couldn't tell who was running through the woods. I never got a clear look at the person."

"But that's what the sheriff said."

"Did the sheriff really tell you that?"

Willow craned her neck toward the bar and motioned to the waitress who waved and came back over to the table.

"Hey, Willow. How's the kids?"

"Just as crazy as ever, and getting more that way every day, especially my middle one."

*Older one. Middle one. Didn't she know their names?* Emma thought, wondering what the poor little beagle's name might be.

"So, what'll you have?"

"I'll have a Bud," Willow said.

"You?" The waitress turned to Emma.

"Just the water, thanks. And two pizzas.

"What would you like on the pizzas, Willow?" Emma                                                                    asked.

"I want everything on mine, and lots of meat and triple cheese."

"I'll have one with all veggies, no hot peppers, please," Emma said. The waitress scratched the order on her pad and left.

"Why you so interested in knowing who shot my brother anyway? You don't have nothing to do with this now, except being a witness when they put Tammy away." Willow said.

*I'd like to reach across the table and slap her out of the restaurant, but I'll smile. Okay, no smile and I won't slap her.*

"You never answered my question. Did Sheriff Day tell you what I told her about the person running through the woods?"

Willow looked away. "Forrest told me she told

him."

"Ahhhh, I see. Well Alder swears that Tammy wouldn't do anything like that."

"You don't know nuthin'. Alder's a jerk. All educated and knows everything. He was blinded by her love and still is. Although she never did love him and he had to cheat on her."

"He said he never cheated on her, Willow."

"Well, he's lying. But I don't blame him, don't get me wrong. But when she found out, she went crazy. Bet he didn't tell you that, did he?"

"How'd she find out?"

Willow looked away again.

"Willow, how'd Tammy find out Alder was cheating on her?"

"I seen him and I told Tammy."

"You saw them? Who? How?"

"At the movies. Alder, holding hands and necking with some slut."

"At a *local* theatre? Don't you think Alder would be smarter than that? This is a pretty small town and everyone knows everyone else. If he were going to step out, he could've driven down the road or even taken her to a hotel, not a public place. Did you know the woman he was with?"

"Doesn't matter. I remember I got to the movie late, and saw them and told Tammy."

"You ratted out your own brother?"

"Well, I thought Tammy should know's all. I mean, men cheated on me, so I know how it feels. I thought I'd help her out. What else did you ask me?"

The waitress set a Bud and a glass on the table in front of Willow.

"Thanks. But I don't need no glass."

"Okay. Your pizzas'll be right out" the waitress said and walked away with the glass.

Emma took a deep breath and looked at Willow. "You go to the movies a lot?"

Willow shook her head and took a big swig of beer.

"So, what movie was playing when you saw them?"

"I don't remember. It was a long time ago."

"How long ago?"

Willow looked pained, shrugged, and drank her beer.

"Was the movie actually playing when you saw them? You said you got there late."

"Yeeeaasss. I-was-at-the-movies. It's what they do there – play movies."

*Oh, brother.* "So the theatre was dark and the movie was playing when you got there and you don't remember the movie." Emma said.

Willow snorted. "That's right."

"How far away were they sitting?"

"Up in the back, like they was hiding."

"So you saw your brother with a woman in a totally dark theater?"

Willow stared at her. "Why you asking me all these dumb questions? It ain't none of your business. You said you wasn't no cop."

"I –"

The waitress set two pizzas, a pile of napkins, and two paper plates on the table. The pans barely hit the table before Willow almost knocked her beer over as she lurched for the pizzas and shoved two pieces into her mouth.

"You need anything else?" the waitress asked.

"No. I think that'll do it," Emma answered, smiling up at her.

"Just let me know if you do. I'll come back and check on you in a bit."

"Great. Thank you," Emma said.

The waitress nodded and left.

Willow devoured piece after piece, shoving it in like it was on a conveyer belt; her pizza disappearing fast.

Emma watched Willow eat, trying hard not to frown. *Reminds me of the mogwais eating chicken before midnight in the movie Gremlins. I'd better hurry and get to my pizza before she goes for it.*

"You're a genius," Gary said, patting Charles on the back while his team left the lab much happier than when they'd entered.

Gary shook his head. "You're the best engineer I've ever known and I'm honored to work with you."

Charles gave him a long look. He'd have to let Gary go. He had no choice. "Thank you, Gary. Now, you'll have to excuse me. I have an appointment."

"Certainly. And thank you again," Gary said, beaming.

Charles nodded and left the lab.

"No interruptions please, Kathy," he said as he walked past her desk. Without giving her a chance to do more than nod in reply, he slid into his office and shut the door. He leaned against it and sighed, looked up at the ceiling, smiled, and pumped his arms. "Yes!"

He walked to his desk and picked up his iPhone. A text message waited.

"Looking forward to our dinner tomorrow evening. I'll bring the Atecca. SJ." Atecca had been their favorite wine. Although Charles loved it, he'd not even looked at a bottle since Simon had left.

His heart filled his entire chest and he felt light-headed. It was always the same feeling, no matter the situation. He was going to see Simon Johnson again

135

after nearly four years.

But he was still wounded and angry over the way Simon had simply walked out on him. And now there was Ron to think about. He did care about Ron; he truly did. But just how much—he knew that was about to be tested.

He sat down at his desk and wondered what Emma would say to all this. He had a feeling he knew what her response would be. She'd think he was crazy for even talking with Simon again, let alone agreeing to see him.

But Emma was dealing with her own issues of the heart right now which he'd only seen her go through one other time. She'd fallen in love with an older man that time, too. She always said she found them more mature. Charles thought Emma was simply looking for a father figure. No matter. She'd loved that particular man and he'd ditched her, totally unexpectedly. He and Emma had that type of heartbreak in common.

She'd been devastated, but was much too proud to wallow in it. She'd sworn off romance and relationships after that and worked from early mornings to late into the nights. Later she'd started H.I.T. and worked less, but kayaked more.

Charles admired her for the way she'd hidden her pain, unlike him when Simon left. He'd fallen apart; probably had a breakdown. If it hadn't been for Emma, he wasn't sure he'd have pulled out of it. She was with him every day for months, understanding, listening, supporting, and finally kicking him in the ass to get a grip. That's when they started taking long weekend kayaking trips–the last two, unfortunately, involving shooting.

He'd tried to talk her into dating, but she said she was too busy. And, in all honesty, she was. But he thought she was only trying to fill a void in her heart that wasn't filled by a relationship. He'd done the same thing himself.

Emma was beautiful, tough, and smart. Many men chased her, but she would have none of it. Until now. It would be interesting to see how *she* dealt with Stratton Reeves.

It would be interesting to see how *he* dealt with Simon Johnson.

# CHAPTER 12

Emma sat in her truck and jotted in her notebook. She'd really learned nothing more than what she'd already suspected from Willow. But confirmation is good and she had a new dog, well, probably several new dogs that she'd have to find homes for.

For whatever reason, Willow was convinced her brother was a cheat and Tammy was the one who'd tried to shoot him too. Emma still wasn't convinced of either accusation. But her twenty years as an insurance fraud investigator had taught her one simple lesson—it takes all kinds.

Beside the notes she wrote *L* and circled it—her notation for Liar. She shut the notebook, stuck the pen in the spine, put it back in her purse, and retrieved her phone. She held it in her hand and stared at it. She took a deep breath and hit a number in her speed dial.

"I'm sorry. I'm sorry a million times, but I just cannot go to Europe until after I find out who shot Alder Mycon. Okay? Then we'll go. I promise. Okay? You're a reporter, you understand this. Right?" Emma winced. *Am I begging?*

"Oh, sweetheart, I'm sorry too. I shouldn't have assumed you would drop your life for me on nothing more than a whim."

"Are you still at the B&B?"

"I am. I wouldn't leave you. When will you be back? I miss you." Stratton said into Emma's ear.

"I'll be there soon."

"And we'll make up?"

Emma smiled. "Yes. We'll make up."

"Good. But can we eat first? Robert and Clara are fixing a fine dinner for us. They saved us a bottle of their best *Côtes du Rhone,* your favorite."

She rolled her eyes. This man was such a romantic – albeit a hungry one. But she liked it. In fact, she was frightened as to how much she liked it. "Sounds good."

"Find out anything more today?" he asked.

"I'll fill you in when I get there."

"Drive safe."

"Okay." She ended the call and tossed the cell in the console. As she started to pull out of Jerry's parking lot, it buzzed. She stopped, put the truck in park, picked up her cell and checked the number. "Unknown." A flash of heat when through her. *Surely not Simon Johnson again.* She hit the talk key and put the phone to her ear.

"Hello?"

"Is this Emma Haines?"

The voice sounded familiar, but she couldn't place it. "Yes, who's this?"

"This is Jebediah Pierce."

"Well, hello there. How are you?"

"I'm just fine. Umm, I was wondering if we could go out. You know, maybe go to eat or a movie or something."

"I'd love to go out. When were you thinking?"

"How about tomorrow night? I can pick you up."

"Tomorrow's great. Why don't we just meet someplace."

"Yeah. Okay. Where do you want to meet?"

She almost said Jerry's. She could eat one of their pizzas every day. "You choose. I've been gone too long to remember what's around."

"Well, how about that bar where we met? You remember where it is, right? They have really good hamburgers, unless you're one of them people that don't like meat or something."

"You're funny. I love burgers. What time should I meet you there?"

"Eight o'clock? That okay? Then we can go to a movie or something. That okay?"

"Sure. Sounds good. I'll see you then, Jebediah."

"Call me Jeb."

"Okay, Jeb. Bye-bye."

She hit the end key and headed toward Willow's to pick up her new dog, a dog-she had no idea what she was going to do with, except find her and the puppies good homes.

"We were thinking of getting a dog soon, but we weren't counting on a pregnant one." Robert said, scratching Lucky's ears. Emma had brought the beagle from Willow's and Robert and Clara had fallen in love with her and named her. Emma was ecstatic.

"I'd keep her if I could, but Murray would have to approve and I doubt that would happen. I would've found a home for her and the pups, eventually. But I'm so glad you're going to keep her. She seems to fit right in. Alexander even seems to like her." The cat had sniffed Lucky shortly after she'd arrived and rubbed on her and left. Alexander was hiding somewhere, probably mulling over this new intruder: Friend or foe?

Emma turned back to her plate. "I can't remember when I've had quiche like this," she said, spearing the last bite from her plate.

"It certainly was wonderful," Stratton said as Clara cleared the table.

"Are you positive? Because you're the only taste testers we have right now besides each other. More people aren't supposed to check in until the weekend. Then we'll add them to our panel," Clara said, picking up Emma's plate. "Stratton tells us you two are going to Europe."

Emma glanced at him. He hid his lower face under a napkin and squinted his eyes at her.

"Yes. We are. And he's doing all the planning and he's paying for everything. We're staying in the best bed and breakfasts the entire time. Why he's even planned for us to do a lot of kayaking while we're there, haven't you, dear," she gave him a wicked smile, picking up her wine glass.

"Absolutely. I've got Rhonda working on it. She said she'd email me the details tomorrow."

"Who's Rhonda?"

"Rhonda is Stratton's secretary. She came with the building. I think they built it around her, in the seventeen-hundreds."

Everyone laughed, including Stratton. "She's my right arm at the newspaper, but she is quite a character."

"You've got that right. But adorable. Clara, you should see this woman. She's as skinny as a stick, about ninety-years-old, and wears bright orange polyester pant-suits every day, with matching plastic jewelry and makeup, doesn't she, honey?"

*Honey.* She'd only called one other man in her life "honey," and he'd shattered her heart. The warning bells clanged in her head. She took a long hit off her wine.

She interrupted him before he could answer. "So, did I mention that I have a date tomorrow night?" she announced.

Stratton gave her a puzzled look through a questioning smile, tilting his head. "Where're we going?"

"We're not. I'm going with someone who knows Forrest Mycon. When I followed Forrest to a bar the

141

other night, the bartender said this guy and Forrest were chatting it up. It had to be a really quick conversation because Forrest was in and out of there too fast to even chug a beer."

"Who is this *date* of yours?" Stratton asked.

"Well, first off, it's not a real date, of course. It's research. Secondly his name's Jebediah Pierce. You know this guy?" Emma asked Robert as he set a tray of flowered China saucers with coffee cups and matching carafe on the table.

"I've heard of him. Can't say I know him."

"Too bad," she said. "I'll have Merek check on him."

"I'll tail you," Stratton said, matter-of-factly before taking a sip of his wine.

"I wouldn't mind at all, but you won't be able to. You'll be busy. I have an assignment for you."

"For me?" Stratton pointed to himself. "And what is that?"

"Robert, do you happen to know when and where Willow does her grocery shopping?"

"As a matter of fact, I do. Thursday mornings at Grocery Barn. I ride my cart like a scooter away from her when I see her coming with her screaming tribe. Why on earth would you want to know that?"

"Because Stratton is going grocery shopping for you there in the morning and will ask the lovely Willow Mycon out for din-din tomorrow night."

"What?" They both nearly yelled in unison.

"Yep. That's your assignment, Mr. Reeves, and you *will* choose to accept it."

Lucky barked and followed Robert into the kitchen, his laughter floating through the air behind him.

It was eight-thirty on Thursday morning as Stratton strolled through Grocery Barn, looking at the candy. He'd been there for about an hour and had already purchased all the items on Robert's shopping list. From what Emma and the Shaws had told him, he doubted he'd find Willow in the produce section, at least not for very long. He heard them before he saw them.

"She hit me."

"I did not."

"Maaaaahmmmmmmmmmmmmmm! Billy put cereal in the cart and you told him not to."

"I did not. He did it."

"Shut up! All of you," Willow yelled.

Stratton turned to see a frustrated looking, large woman, in a torn, red jacket, gray sweat pants, and worn tennis shoes, with five just as nicely dressed kids in tow. One was in the cart, two were hanging off the cart, and the other two were trailing behind. One was picking his nose and wiping his findings on nearly everything on the shelves as he passed.

Stratton sagged with dread and made a mental note to buy a bottle of hand sanitizer before he left. *Touché, Emma*, he thought to himself and snickered under his breath.

The woman stopped beside him and reached for a bag of Snickers. He quickly went for the same bag, purposely brushing her hand.

"Oh, excuse me. I'm so terribly sorry," he said in that voice that could melt glaciers and turn the sun to ice.

Willow looked at him, mouth hanging open. "Ain't no problem. No problem at all."

"Mooooooaaaaaaahhhhhmmmmmmmmmmmmm,"one of the children squealed so loud, Stratton nearly jumped.

"You shut up right now and go fetch some bacon. Take your brother and sisters with you," she yelled at the tallest boy in the group.

The boy looked at Stratton, wiped his nose on the back of his hand, and ran down the aisle. The others followed except for the little girl who sat in the cart like a tiny Buddha with a dirty face. She looked up at Stratton with huge brown eyes, smiled, and pointed at him.

"Daddy," she yelled. Stratton nearly fainted, but instead smiled and turned to Willow.

"Oh, she says that to every man she sees. She don't mean nothing by it, I mean…"

"No harm at all. She's a lovely child. What's her name?"

"Esther."

"Well, hello, there, Esther. My name is Stratton." He turned to Willow and extended his hand. "Stratton Reeves. And you are?"

Willow stared at him, not moving. "Name's Willow."

"Willow. What a lovely name. I'm from out of town and stopped in to pick up a few groceries. I'm renting a place while I'm here on business. I'm so pleased to meet you. You have such a lovely brood."

"Brood?"

"Children. Your children are lovely."

"They been called a lot of things, but never lovely," she pulled up her sweatpants and laughed.

Esther kept yelling, "Daddy. Daddy. Daddy." Stratton wanted to run.

Stratton had done a lot of crazy things in his career to get a story, but this had to be one of the worst. *Emma is really going to pay for this.*

"Well, Willow. Are you from around here?"

She stared at him for a few seconds. "Yeah."

"I was wondering if you could tell me about any good restaurants in the area. Even after buying all this food, I just feel like going out this evening."

Willow gazed off down the aisle then back at Stratton. She smiled, dropped her chin, licked her lips, smoothed her greasy hair, and jutted her hip. Stratton nearly gasped.

"Well, I reckon there's a few places around here. What kind of food you want?"

Stratton's mind whirred as he looked at her. "Burgers and fries. I love a good burger and fries. And steak."

"Well, you could go to the Blue Caboose. They got both and they're real good."

Emma had told him to go anywhere except the Blue Caboose. That's where she and Jebediah were meeting. He smiled.

"Well, you know, after I think about it a minute, I haven't had seafood in a long time. I noticed a seafood place on the way into town. How's their food?"

"It's good. I only ate there a couple times. It's pretty expensive for me, but probably okay for someone like you."

Stratton looked down at the floor before he raised his head with his best smile. "You know, I never do this, but may I ask you a question?"

"What?"

"Well, I love children and I miss my grandchildren. I've been traveling for weeks and need some good conversation at dinner. Would you and your family like to join me tonight? My treat."

Willow frowned. "What do you mean? You want to take me and my kids to dinner?"

"Yes. That's exactly what I mean. I would enjoy it. Really. And your husband too."

"I ain't got no husband."

"Oh. Well, then. If you and your children would like to go out tonight. Or, perhaps, if you're not seeing anyone, what about just you and me? Like I said, I never do this, but I've been craving conversation and I would love to hear about the area. You said you're from here and I'll bet you could tell me a great deal about Chillicothe."

Willow's jaw dropped. "You asking me out on a date?" She pointed at herself and shook her head in disbelief.

"Well, yes. I suppose I am. It's not a problem for me. You see, I'm single. I've been widowed for several years. I'm here on business. It would be lovely if you were to join me for dinner, Willow."

Willow's cheeks flushed. "*You* want to go out with *me*?"

"Yes, I would enjoy it very much. You seem like such a friendly person. And we could meet at the restaurant. I know you don't know me at all, so you could drive there and go home if you didn't care for my company. What do you say? Tonight at eight? Meet at the restaurant?"

"Okay. I reckon I can do that." She patted her hair and smoothed her jacket. She looked up and smiled. She had several teeth missing.

Esther watched the conversation with a fist in her mouth.

"Fine. Sounds wonderful. I'm looking forward to it. See you then."

"Okay."

Esther began screaming then abruptly stopped. A strange, strong odor rose from the cart.

Stratton looked at her, nodded at Willow, turned, and pushed his cart as fast as he could without running toward the checkout.

"I told you, Tammy didn't shoot me, I swear. She would never do it. You have to find who shot me. Can you do that?" Alder's voice pleaded through Emma's phone. "I don't know who else to turn to."

She shifted her cell to her other ear and jotted notes in her notebook. She read her notes over and over when she was working on a case, until the picture became clearer and clearer and she could figure out the ending.

"I told you I'd try. And I will. But why are you so sure? Everything's pointing straight at her. Alder, come on. They even found the gun that fired the bullet in her closet."

"I'm telling you, she didn't do it. You met her. Do you think she'd do it?"

Emma didn't answer. She'd told him her story about meeting Tammy, and reminded him of the Jeep and the coat. "Look, I'll try to see her today and talk to her again, okay? I'm looking into it."

Alder went on as Stratton walked through the dining room doorway. He sat down at the table across from her. She listened, jotted more notes, and mouthed "Alder Mycon" toward Stratton.

He nodded and held the bridge of his nose and closed his eyes. Emma had already learned that wasn't a good sign.

"Look, I'll let you know what's going on. I need to go now, Alder. I'll be in touch. Right. Okay. Bye."

She closed the notepad and theatrically placed her cell on top of it. She sat back and crossed her arms and legs.

"Well, you don't look too happy. What's up?" She grinned.

"Emma Haines, you're a little devil."

"So? You have a hot date tonight?" She snickered.

"I most certainly do. How could you do this to me?"

She stood, walked around the table, and put her arms around his neck. His silver neck chain caught the light as he leaned back to look up at her. She kissed him. "Want to go upstairs and I'll apologize?" She asked on his lips. He rubbed her arms. He stood and they kissed a few more times.

"Well, alright. But this will take a great deal of apologizing, young lady."

"No problem," she said as she took his hand and led him toward the staircase.

"Merek, I need you to get everything you can for me on a guy here in Chillicothe named Jebediah Pierce."

"Right, Miss H. What is the spelling of the first name?"

"Not sure, just try several. I need all you can get on him before seven this evening."

"Hold on."

Merek tapping his keyboard came through the earpiece followed by a few seconds of silence.

"No Facebook pages or websites with any name like that."

"That doesn't surprise me. See if he has a record. That won't surprise me either. Call me back before seven. Okay?"

"Sure thing.

"Miss H. I need to talk to you about something."

"Okay. What?"

"Oh, nothing."

"Tell her," a woman's voice came across the phone. "Someone there with you?"

"I need to talk to you when you return. When will that be?"

"Tell her now, Merek," the woman's voice ordered. "Tell her right now or I will."

"Miss H., I gotta scram."

The call went dead.

She stared at the phone and shrugged.

"Something wrong?" Stratton asked.

"I don't know. Merek must be having an argument with one of his blondes. He only dates blondes and he's always scrammin' and never says goodbye. Maybe it's a Polish thing or something," she said to Stratton who lay beside her in bed. She placed her cell on the side table. "You hungry?"

"Funny you should mention that. I am."

"We'll go raid the fridge."

She gave him a peck on the cheek, got out of bed, walked across the room into the bathroom, and shut the door. A few seconds later the shower came on.

Stratton sat up on his pillows, picked up his Samsung from the side table and called Rhonda. "Hello, Rhonda. How are things there?"

"Oh, Stratton, fine, just fine. But I think Maggie is really missing you. Missing you awful bad. I mean, she's not hurt or anything like that. She's a good dog, just fine, don't get me wrong. But she's not eating all her food and that has me a little worried. Not a lot, just a little, mind you. I mean she's not skinny, but I don't think it's right, her not eating and all and—"

"You're probably right. She misses me. I miss you both too," he interrupted. Usually, you had to interrupt Rhonda or you'd never stand a chance of having a conversation.

"Oh, my. Now, that's just so sweet of you to say

that. So sweet. Well, we miss you too. When will you be home? I'm not rushing you or anything. You know I love staying in this big ole beautiful house of yours. Gives me a break from Cole, I'll give you that. Did I tell you what he did last week? Well, never mind. It doesn't matter. I'm just glad I wasn't there to see it. He had no right to paint the kitchen while I was gone. I mean, really. It's not like he couldn't have waited until I got home, could he? Well, anyway. It was just awful. When are you coming home?"

"I'm not sure. Maybe I'll come down and get Maggie and bring her up here. I'm helping Emma on a case, so I don't know when I'll be back."

"Oh, my. Well, that'd be alright and—"

He jumped in and told Rhonda about it.

"Well, that's just awful. Plum awful. Miss Emma could've been hurt. That's just awful, Stratton. Now, you know she's got no business chasing those nasty types of people. No woman should be doing things like that. Especially a pretty little thing like Miss Emma. You ought not let her do that, Stratton. You need to get her back home. She needs to stop that."

"Well, you know her well enough to know that she won't stop until she's solved it. I guess I'll stay here until she kicks me out."

"Now, Stratton. Appears Miss Emma has no intention of kicking you out. She seems awful sweet on you, just awful sweet. And from what I can tell you feel the same way. You can't hide nothing from me, no you can't. Not a thing. You know me better than that. When are you two getting married?"

"Now, that's a good question. I'll let you know when I know the answer."

"Did you ask her? Maybe she's waiting for you to ask her, I mean, give her a big purdy ring and get on your knee and ask her. Did you?"

"Not directly. I want to take her to Europe and ask her over there. Less chance she can run. But we'll have to solve this situation here first."

"Oh, my. Now if you get married, you're not moving up there are you? I mean, it's none of my business, but it is, so I just gotta ask you, flat out. Flat out, Stratton, because it's been on my mind. Weighing heavy on mind since you and Miss Emma have been getting so close. Not that I don't want you to. I do. I do. It's just, I gotta ask you right flat out. You're not selling the paper are you?"

Stratton chuckled. "Don't you worry, Rhonda. No matter what happens, you'll have a job at the paper."

"I surely hope she comes here to live. I don't want to lose either one of you. I mean, I really don't want to work for no one else, really. Not really. I been working here since I was in high school and I just don't want to work for no one else or have to find another job. And I'm never going to retire. No, I'll tell you. You retire, you die. You just die. I've seen people do it. They just retire and die. Now, it's none of my business, you know. But you need to bring Miss Emma down here and live. You two get married and come right back down here, I tell you. Right back home."

"Well, all I have to do is talk her into it, but we'll see. Right now isn't the time to bring that up and if you talk to her, don't you dare say a word about this."

"Oh, Stratton. I would never do such a thing. You know that. Not a word would I breathe to her about what you told me. You know me better than that. And—"

"And don't tell anyone else either. Okay?"

She didn't answer.

"Rhonda? Are you still there?"

"Stratton, there's someone here. I need to go."

"Who is it?" he asked.

"It's Officer Lawrence. I'd best talk to him."
"What's he—?"
The phone clicked off in his ear.

# CHAPTER 13

"Got your info, Miss H."

"Merek, that's quick work. It's only two."

"I am, as they say, a bang-whiz."

Emma laughed. "A whiz-bang. Anyway, what do you have?" She pulled out her notebook and flipped to the page she'd started on Jebediah Pierce.

"I tell you first, Calvin Nelson called for you. He even asked me where you are. First nice, then he demanded that I tell him."

"And?"

"Like I would tell him." He laughed.

"He's called me five times. I haven't answered. What'd he want? Did he have questions about the project?"

"He didn't ask me any questions. He sounded like he really wanted to talk to you, not me. Told me to call you and tell you to call him immediately. He said it's personal."

"Like I'll do that. Anyway, forget Calvin. What do you have on Pierce?

"Jebediah James Pierce." He spelled Jebediah, "is fifty-seven years of age, has a job for past thirty-eight years at the Glassgow Steel Plant in South Bloomtown, fifteen miles from Chillicothe. Works on the assembly line making beams for buildings. Lives in Chillicothe on Walker Avenue with his mother.

"Divorced five years ago, no kids. Wife appears to have left town. He's never owned property, always rented. Drives a 2003 brown Saturn four-door. License ALT230."

"That's my guy," she said.

"Four tickets, all speeding, one DUI over five years past. Nothing else. No other arrest record," Merek reported through his Polish accent.

"Hard to believe if he hangs with Forrest Mycon. Anyway, great work, Merek. You know I couldn't live without you."

"I do know this, Miss H. You tell me, many times and I do believe you. And I know it is true."

"Right. Anything else?"

"Yes. There is something else. He had his picture on the front of *The Bloomburg Banister* newspaper of him holding the head up of a twelve-point buck deer last November."

"You're right. That is something else."

"And I am also wondering when you might think you will be returning as we need to discuss a very important matter."

"What is it, Merek?"

"I cannot say over the phone. It is complicated. Hey, Miss H, I need to scram."

And he did.

Emma sat with Tammy and Taylor Eastland at their kitchen table drinking a Pepsi on ice from a crystal tumbler. She rarely drank soft drinks, but it tasted good.

The clock said it was two thirty, which reminded Emma that she'd forgotten to call Charles. After she'd talked to Merek, she'd called Tammy who'd agreed to see her so she hurried over. She had a four o'clock appointment with Alder and, later, her date with Jebediah Pierce. It was turning into a busy Thursday.

Tammy wore a green sweat suit and a pair of neon

blue Nikes. She held a tissue in her hands that she was tearing to shreds with her perfectly French manicured nails. Even dressed like this with a puffy red face, her lipstick and makeup were perfect. She looked both professional and a bit on the sexy side. *Disgusting*, Emma thought.

Taylor was bald and quite handsome. Emma could see why Tammy would want to marry this guy. He reached over and took Tammy's hand.

"Our lawyer told us not to discuss this case with anyone, but Tammy agreed to talk to you because, well, she said she likes you and trusts you. Right, sweetheart?"

Tammy nodded and started crying and shaking her head again. "I didn't shoot Alder. Why would I do that? I haven't shot that rifle for years."

"Who knows you have that gun?" Emma asked.

She shrugged and sniffed. "I don't know. Taylor, of course," she said, nodding toward him. "Other than Taylor, I have no idea. Why?"

"Alder?"

"Well, yes. He knew I was a sharpshooter and that I kept it. It was my favorite. We used to go out to shoot in the quarry sometimes."

"Has the rifle always been in the same closet in this house where the sheriff found it?"

"Yes. I put it in there when I moved in. I haven't shot it in years," she repeated.

"And no one knows that rifle was in that closet besides you and Taylor?"

"No."

Emma looked at Taylor. Nothing. Not a flinch. She turned back to Tammy.

"Do you have a cleaning woman or anyone else that could've seen that rifle in the closet? Visitors, anyone?"

"Oh, this is all so repetitive. Sheriff Day asked me all these questions too."

"I know. And I'm sorry. But I have to ask them too." Emma gave her a sincere concerned look.

"I have some friends over for poker on Thursday nights, but I'm sure none of them ever looked in that closet," Taylor said.

"They wouldn't have hung a coat or anything in there, seen the rifle and taken it?" Emma asked Taylor.

"If someone steals, they're not my friend. Besides, the closet where the rifle was kept is in our bedroom. Not the guest closet in the hallway. And how would they get it back in the closet?"

Emma had thought of that a long time ago and admired Taylor's thinking, although it didn't help either one of them. Emma quickly wondered if Taylor suspected Tammy and decided she needed to talk to him alone at some point. And, he was also the only other person that knew about the rifle. "That's the million dollar question, isn't it?"

They sat in silence for a few seconds before Emma asked, "Do either of you know a man named Jebediah Pierce?"

"Know him. Not well. What about him?" Taylor answered.

"Has he ever been in your house?"

Taylor gave Emma a long look. "Why?"

"Just curious. Has he?"

"He's been over to play poker a few times over the years. Why?"

"When's the last time he was here?"

"A couple of weeks ago. Why?"

Emma stared at him. "I think he's a friend of Forrest's. Has Forrest ever been here playing poker?"

"Well, of course, not. I wouldn't have drug trash like that near my property." Taylor was indignant, as he continued. "But I can't control who others associate with. Jeb was invited by another player. We were short and they came together, him and Mike. I think it was Mike. Yes, Mike brought him."

"What's Mike's last name?" Emma asked.

"Legkey. Mike Legkey. Works at a factory a few miles out of town. What about this Jeb man?"

"I'm not sure, just checking out everything I can think of. You mentioned Forrest was into drugs?"

"Everyone knows he smokes marijuana and rumors are he's into coke and crack and who knows what else. It's all the same to me. Drug trash is drug trash," Taylor said.

"Look, I'll need a list of everyone, name, address, phone, and where they work, if you know, that's been in this house in the past, say, six months or so, including your poker-playing buddies. And I do mean everyone."

"Why? What do you intend to do with it?" Taylor asked.

"Check them out," Emma replied.

"And how on earth do you intend to do that?" he asked.

"I have my ways." *I also have Merek and Joey.* "Could you pull the list together for me by tomorrow?"

"I don't know. I suppose. I'll try."

"Good. I'll call before I come to pick it up; the sooner, the better." She turned to Tammy.

"Have *you* ever known Forrest Mycon to be in this house?"

Tammy shook her head and made a sort of animal squeal before she started bawling again, gasping for air like a little red-lipped guppy.

Taylor patted her hand. "Honey, now don't get upset. You know what the doctor told us."

Tammy nodded. "I know. I'll calm down."

"Doctor?" Emma asked.

"I'm pregnant," she said, smiling through her tears. "And now my baby's mother is going to have a record for attempted murder. I still can't believe this is happening. Oh, Miss Haines, you've got to help us."

Taylor turned to Emma. "Ms. Haines, maybe you can help us, but I don't want her upset. I can certainly afford to hire a private detective, but Tammy insisted on talking to you first. And, honestly, I don't really know of any around here. I've never had the need for one. But I guess the police or someone could refer me to one. Anyway, she wanted to talk to you, but I think this has been enough."

"And why did you want to talk to me, a total stranger? I'm curious," she asked Tammy.

She gulped back more tears. "Because Alder trusts you. I called him when I got out on bail. He knows it wasn't me. He said he thinks you don't think it was me either and you're an investigator of some kind and he said you could help me."

Emma looked at Taylor. No response. He just looked at Tammy.

"Oh, it's alright. Alder and Taylor are acquaintances. It's a small town, that's just the way it is. There's no hard feelings or anything between any of us," Tammy explained. Emma looked at Taylor for a reaction to her calling Alder. Nothing.

He turned to Emma. "That's right, Ms. Haines. Alder's a good man. What happened between him and Tammy is none of my concern. We all know that Tammy and I have our own lives now."

"Does Alder know about your pregnancy?"

Tammy nodded. "I told him when I called and he was so happy for Taylor and me. He truly was."

"Well, that's good. Oh, and congratulations."

"Thank you." They looked at each other and beamed– as much as they could, given the situation. The phone rang and Taylor leaned over to give her a peck on the cheek before he got up from the chair to answer it.

"Excuse me. I'll take this in the other room," he said and left through a large archway leading to a corridor.

Tammy and Emma watched him leave and sat in silence for several seconds before Tammy turned to Emma.

"I wasn't going to tell you this, but I will. I divorced Alder because he couldn't have children. That's the real reason we're not together. I always wanted a family and he just couldn't..."

"Oh. I see. Well, what about..."

Tammy shook her head. "He refused to go through that and frankly, I didn't want to go through it either. It got to be such an issue between us that it finally broke the marriage.

"Many people thought I ran out and got the first man I could find. Some of them know about Alder. But that's not what happened. I really didn't know Taylor that well, him being so much older than me. But I met him at a real estate banquet and I fell in love with him. I really did. He loves me and he always wanted children too. He'd never married and well, there you have it.

"Honestly, I care about Alder, but I was never in love with him like he was with me. I think he'd do anything for me. Even watch me marry another man and have his children because he knew how much I wanted a family. He really is a good man, Ms. Haines."

"Alder told me you divorced because you wanted a career and he wanted a down-home farm girl, basically. I can understand why he wouldn't tell me this."

Tammy nodded and sniffled. "Yeah. It's not something men go around talking about. In fact, I only told a few people. I felt horrible about the divorce, but he said he loved me and wanted me to be happy. "

Even with tears streaming down her face and

through everything she'd been through in the past several hours, her makeup and hair still looked perfect.

*How do some women do that?*

Taylor walked back into the room. Emma thought the timing was a little too perfect and figured he simply chose to avoid the conversation.

"Can I get you anything else, Ms. Haines? Another Pepsi?"

"No, no. Thank you. I'm fine. I just have a few more questions then I'll let you both get some rest."

Emma turned back to Tammy. "Willow and Forrest are convinced that you shot Alder. They swear to it and sadly, as you know, there's a lot of evidence pointing to you, especially that rifle found in your closet. Tammy, if you didn't do it, how did that rifle get back in your closet after it'd been fired?"

"I don't know. But I do know, those two always hated me. Since the second Alder and I were married. They would do anything to ruin me and Alder. They're just worthless pieces of trash. I can't believe Alder is even related to them."

"You're not answering my question. If you expect me to help you, you're going to have to be totally straight up with me. How did that rifle get back in your closet?"

Tears spilled from Tammy's eyes and she dropped her head in her hands. "I don't know. I don't know. God, help me. I didn't do it."

On her way down the driveway, Emma looked under Tammy's shining red Jeep one more time. Clean as a pin. She climbed in her dirty Tacoma and drove toward Alder's.

Before she'd left the Eastland's, Emma had asked Tammy about Willow ratting out Alder about his cheating. Tammy said that by then, they'd already seen an attorney and Tammy really didn't care one way or the other if Alder was seeing someone else. They'd agreed their marriage was over. In fact, she'd hoped Willow was telling the truth for once. But she'd known Willow was lying. Emma wasn't surprised when Tammy went on to tell her, "Willow's known to never tell the truth."

She had a weight of sadness in her chest for Alder and Tammy, even though she knew nothing about marriage or wanting children.

Emma was a free spirit, thriving on work and kayaking, not buying into the promises of romance and marriage. After having been dumped once, she'd decided not to ever put herself in that position again. Hah!

She had no siblings, so Murray, Merek, Charles, and Mary, had always been her chosen family since her parents had died over a decade ago. For the sixteen years she'd known Simon, she'd considered him family too, but that came to an abrupt end when he walked out on Charles to move to Spain and left her with the job of putting Charles back together.

She loved her life. Simple. Uncomplicated. No strings. But since she'd met Stratton Reeves, her heart was often in a battle with her head and she didn't care for the struggle. In fact, she despised it. But it was always there, giving her stomach flips, taking away her control.

Emma's head rattled with thoughts of Alder, Tammy, Taylor, Willow, Forrest, Jebediah, Charles, Merek, Joey, Mary, and Calvin Nelson. She thought about how people tend to create such complicated lives.

"What tangled webs we do indeed weave," she said to her truck's windshield as she drove up the long lane to Alder's house.

Emma sat in Alder's great room in one of the four overstuffed brown leather chairs. Brass rivets ran along the upholstery line. It was soft and comfortable. The chairs reminded her of the ones sitting around Stratton's desk in his office at the *Sandstone Post* in West Virginia. Her stomach did that little flip. *Damn it.*

The room was wood, wood, wood, everywhere wood, complete with beamed ceilings and plank wooden floors. Pictures of outdoor scenes hung on the walls. Beer steins of every shape and size covered the mantel above a stone fireplace that reminded her of Mary's. Streaks of afternoon sun streamed in and fell across the long, matching leather couch. Emma thought it'd be nice to lie down and take a nap on it.

Coals glowed in the fireplace. She stared at them, wishing she were home with Murray in front of the small gas fireplace in her condo. And she would be as soon as she cracked this case. Or would she be in Europe? The thought caused her to squirm.

"Nice room. You do this yourself?" She looked around.

Alder shook his head, but said nothing.

"Tammy?"

He nodded.

He stared into the fire. "She and Taylor are going to have a baby. Did you know that?"

Emma nodded. "I just came from their house."

He glanced at her as a flame shot high up the chimney. He got up and tossed three split logs on the fire from a large wood pile sitting to the right of the fireplace. He sat back down and they stared at the fire.

"Can I get you anything? Coffee, tea, Coke? Something to eat?" Alder asked.

"No thanks, I'm fine," she replied as her stomach

growled. She thought of the delicious quiche Robert and Clara had prepared for them last night and how she and Stratton had taken a second bottle of wine upstairs and finished it off throughout the evening. Her stomach growled again. Alder glanced at her and smiled.

"Let me fix you a sandwich."

"No. No. I'm fine, thanks. I'll be eating a big dinner soon." *With Jeb*, she thought. She glanced at her watch. "Look, I want to help you, but the evidence against Tammy's pretty strong, especially that rifle."

"She didn't do it. How many times do I have to tell you? Do you think she did it?"

"Doesn't matter what I think."

"It does if you're going to help her."

"If she didn't shoot at you, Alder, who did?"

He shrugged. "I have no idea."

"Could it have been Taylor?"

"Taylor? Why would he want to shoot me?"

"You'd know that better than me."

Emma looked at the fire. She started thinking about a case that took her and Joey about three years to solve. But they did. They never lost hope that their hunch was right and later it panned out. She had that same feeling now. She propped her elbows on the chair arms and rested her chin on her intertwined fingers.

"Alder, why are your brother and sister so certain Tammy's the shooter?"

"I don't know. Like I've told you. I really don't know them, but they always hated Tammy."

"So I've heard. Why is that?"

"I'm not really sure, but Tammy's smart, pretty, outgoing, has money. Everything they're not."

"They don't like you very much either. That right?"

Alder shrugged. "They were mad when dad gave me the farm. Guess they're probably still not too happy about that. But we weren't ever close. We were always so different. I got good grades in school and they rarely showed up for classes. Always in different directions."

Emma sat and thought that over for a few seconds. Something was bugging her about that white envelope in Jeb's front pocket. "I have a meeting tonight with Jebediah Pierce. You said you don't know him. You sure?"

Alder thought about it then shook his head. "No."

Emma turned away from him and watched the fire. She thought of all the kayaking trips she and Charles had taken, afterward sitting around a fire late at night, becoming hypnotized by the flames, sharing each other's company in silence for hours. She sank a little lower in the chair.

Emma and Alder watched the fire. It crackled and came to life, catching the bottom log. He got up and poked it with a large poker for what seemed like hours before he put the poker back in its rack and sat down again.

"I followed your brother to the Blue Caboose Saturday night and the bartender told me he'd been talking to a man named Jebediah Pierce," she said.

"Lanny told you that?" Alder looked back at the fire and smiled. "That bar's been in town forever. My dad and mom used to go there and shoot pool on dates, before they were married. It's changed hands a million times, but everyone says it still looks the same."

"I can believe that. Who's Lanny?"

"Lanny Klinn. The bartender. Kind of small guy, younger, beard, curly blonde hair and tattoos. Looks like a biker?"

"That was the guy."

"He owns it now. Not sure how long he's had it. Taylor would know."

"Taylor Eastland?"

"Yeah, Taylor. The last 'For Sale' sign I saw in front

of it had his name on it."

Emma stared at him. He had that same look on his face that she'd seen on Charles's for months after Simon had left him. Sadness. Defeat. Heartbreak.

"You talk to Tammy often?" she asked.

He shook his head. "No need to. I just talked to her after they got married, I bump into her and Taylor around town, but not much, and the other day when she called me after she got out on bail. I stay here on the farm, mostly."

Emma checked her watch and stood. "Look, Alder, you've helped me a lot, but I need to run." She stood and headed toward the door. "Can you call me if you think of anything else?"

"Yeah, sure thing. But I don't know what I said that helped."

Emma got in her truck, dug her cell out of her purse, and punched a number on the keypad.

Merek answered on the second ring. "H.I.T. How may I give you anything your heart desires this lovely afternoon, Miss H.?"

"By getting me what I need pretty quick."

*"Dobry wieczor."*

"Yeah. Whatever you said."

"It means good evening, Miss H."

"Oh. Right. Good evening, Merek. Hey, look, I need you to check out a bar owner down here, pronto. Owns a bar called The Blue Caboose. Name's Lanny Klinn. Not sure how to spell it, but—"

"No worries, Miss H. You do not know how to spell many names."

"If you can get me the information on him before

seven, I'll remember how to spell yours when I write out a bonus check."

"I gotta scram, Miss H."

"Of course, you do," she said after the call ended in her ear.

She tossed the cell in the truck console and headed back to the mall on Bridge Street. She needed a new outfit for her date with Jebediah Pierce.

# CHAPTER 14

Charles paced his house, the boys following him nearly every step. Dinner was warm in the oven. The salad was chilling in the fridge, the wine was breathing, the table was set. Everything was ready. It'd been ready. He'd left work at two o'clock, gone to Weiland's Market and bought everything fresh to prepare, along with a beautiful bouquet of flowers which graced the table in a crystal vase Simon had bought for their twelfth anniversary.

He'd left the boys at Janet's until six-thirty so they wouldn't be in the way as he scrubbed and cleaned, above and beyond what his cleaning company had done just two days prior, before he concentrated on preparing the meal.

The clock on the Viking double-oven read 7:15 p.m. Simon was to arrive at eight.

Charles walked into the great room and sat on the couch. He ran his fingers through his hair and closed his eyes. His palms were sweating. He took a deep breath and thought it funny how he saved a satellite from crashing to Earth yesterday without flinching, yet the thought of seeing Simon again was nearly hurling him into orbit.

The boys wandered into the room, tails wagging. Cecil jumped on the couch, made a few turns, curled into a tight ball, and, smiling, faced Charles. Cleo and Sam flopped down at Charles's feet. "Alright, listen up, guys."

Tails thumped. The dogs' brown eyes gave him their full attention. They looked like brothers from the same litter, but in fact, he and Simon had adopted them from the Labrador Rescue at various times.

Sam was the oldest at ten, followed by Cecil at seven, and Cleo was five. Charles gave Cleo a pat and thought about the day he and Simon went to pick him up with Sam and Cecil in the SUV. They'd had lunch at Smith's Deli on High Street. It seemed that all four of them were happy to be getting another family member. Little did Charles know that Simon would walk out on all of them about a year later.

"Simon will be here soon and I want you all to be on your best behavior. Do you understand?"

Cecil yawned. Sam tucked his head under his tail and Cleo barked. "That's right, Cleo. You understand, don't you?"

Cleo wagged his tail before he got up and strolled into the kitchen to lap water from his bowl.

Charles got up from the couch, walked down the long hallway and into the master bedroom. He checked himself in the full-length mirror for the tenth time. He had on a new pair of chinos, crisply ironed, and a yellow shirt, Simon's favorite color.

He wore a splash of the cologne Simon had given him for Christmas four years ago. Charles had no premonition whatever then that it would be their last Christmas together. *Or would it?*

He stared at himself in the mirror. He lifted his arms in front of him. His hands were shaking.

His iPhone vibrated in his pocket. He pulled it out and checked the screen, frowned, and let it vibrate three more times before he hit the talk icon.

"Hello, Ron."

"Hey, there. Look, I know you have plans, but you said you wanted to talk to me, but you didn't call. I figured you were caught up at work. So, I thought maybe I'd catch you before your appointment."

"Tonight simply isn't a good night to talk. I'm sorry." There was silence. He took a deep breath and exhaled slowly. "Ron, I'm seeing Simon. He's in town and is coming over for dinner. I'm sorry I didn't tell you and I do want to talk with you about all this, but... I just..."

A heavy silence crossed the air waves.

"I see."

More silence.

"I won't keep you then," Ron finally said.

"Ron, wait..."

But the phone went dead in Charles's ear.

"Sweetheart, are you really wearing *that* to meet this strange man who may be a killer?" Stratton had both hands on his hips and a frown on his face. Emma wore a mini-skirt, a tight tube-top, black hose, and red stilettoes.

"I went shopping today on my way back from Alder's. What? You don't like it? Besides, Jebediah is not a killer. He flunked out on that, if he did, in fact, shoot at Alder Mycon. Anyway, it looks like Tammy shot Alder. But I do think Forrest went in that bar Saturday night and gave Jeb an envelope with some cash in it for something. Drugs, I'd guess. I'd guess Jeb's a dealer. I'm going to find out." She turned back to the mirror on the antique dresser and applied more blood-red lipstick.

"You mentioned the envelope the other day."

"It was sticking out of his breast pocket when I talked to him. Looked like it had something thick in it and the bartender said Forrest had been talking to Jeb.

Charles and I both watched Forrest go in and out of that bar pretty quick. I think Forrest gave him that envelope and it probably had a wad of cash in it, or maybe what Jeb thought was a wad of cash, and Forrest split before Jeb had a chance to look at it. Maybe. I don't know. That envelope and Forrest's quick exit after talking with Jeb has to be connected to this shooting. I feel it."

"So there. That's even more reason why I should follow you. He's a drug dealer and connected to this. Are you *really* going to wear that?"

"What? You don't approve?   Or are you just jealous?"

"It's not that. It's… well, you look like …"

"A hooker?"

"Well, yes. You do. Emma, I believe I should follow you and this man. You don't know who he is and I..."

"Am protective?"

"Very."

"Good. Me, too. Now you go get ready for your date with Willow."

"Alright."

"Now, don't let Willow get the better of you. You don't want to give those kids another sibling."

Stratton shuddered.

Emma gave him a quick look then turned back to spray more hairspray on her hair. She coughed and waved her hand in front of her face.

"Why do women do this to themselves?"

He walked behind her and began kissing the back of her neck.

"Stop that. We don't want to be late for our dates."

She turned and they kissed as he pulled her toward the bed.

170

Stratton stepped out of his shining, black Silverado pickup in the parking lot of the seafood restaurant. He wore polished black cowboy boots and a long, black trench coat. His jeans were creased and his striped blue cotton shirt was crisply starched. Not one silver hair on his head was out of place and he smelled of light cologne.

Willow arrived in a ten-year-old, rusted green Chevy van that looked like it'd been through a nuclear attack. Stratton waved and smiled. She jerked the van to a stop and lumbered toward him through the parking lot. He considered sprinting toward his truck, but stood fast.

"Willow, it's so nice to see you."

Willow stood and stared at him. "Wow. You look real good. Real good."

"Why thank you. So do you. Shall we go have dinner?"

Willow nodded. "I'm starving."

Her stained nylon sweat suit made swishing sounds as she walked.

Once seated in a booth by a window, they ordered their drinks. Stratton had a Yuengling and Willow a jumbo piña colada. They made small talk about Chillicothe. Not surprisingly, Stratton knew about its history. She knew nothing nor cared. He talked about the Adena mansion and Thomas Worthington while Willow sat slumped over her glass, sucking on a straw, seldom looking up.

By the time their meal arrived, Willow was slurping down her third drink.

*Perfect*, he thought.

"So Willow, tell me more about your family. Do you have brothers and sisters?"

She finally made eye contact with him, briefly,

before looking away. "I ain't got no sisters, just two brothers. One's a rich snot and the other's a no-good druggie. Nothing more to tell."

"Surely there's more than that."

"Why you want to know about them?" she grumbled, sucking up the last of her drink and motioning to the waitress for another. When the waitress arrived at their table, Willow thrust the glass toward her.

"Can you make these stronger? I can't even feel a buzz yet."

The waitress looked at Stratton and he gave her a quick smile and nodded. "No problem. I'll drive the lady home."

The waitress took the glass and left.

"So you wanna take me home, huh?"

"If you're too inebriated to drive, I'll be glad to drive you."

"You sure are a nice man. Real purdy too. Fancy clothes. Fancy truck. Fancy talk. I think we could have another drink at my place. You up for that?"

"Certainly. Sounds enjoyable."

"It sure does," Willow winked at him. Stratton glanced out the window, sighed, and took a sip of the beer he'd originally ordered.

"You can arrange for someone to get your van back to your home tomorrow. Perhaps one of your brothers could bring you."

"Ha! That's a laugh. One ain't no better than the other to me, really. Even though one of them is trying to help me get some money."

"How's that?"

"About time," she said as the waitress placed the fourth piña colada on the table and left.

"What'd you say, sugar?" Willow said as she sucked on her straw.

"I simply asked how your brother was helping you get money."

She eyed him as she took a long drink through the straw. She slammed back against the booth seat, jolting it. Her eyes rolled back in her head as she wiped her mouth with the back of her hand. "Well, I can't talk about it."

Stratton smiled, nodded, and took another small drink of beer, regretting he couldn't chug several of them.

"But I been needing to talk about it with someone besides Forrest. He's such an asshole. You see me and Forrest, that's my older brother, he's thirty-two, he's got a nasty crack habit and he's in for it with his dealer. He needs money or his dealer's gonna cut him off and cut him up, least that's what he says."

"Well now, that is a difficult position. But you say he now has a plan to get money? A lot? Or at least, enough?"

"Yeah. You see, my other brother is the snob who got everything when our Daddy died. The family farm, all the money, *everything*. Then he married that pretty bitch, Tammy. Our daddy cut me and Forrest out of everything. Said we turned into trash. Can you believe that? Left us with nothing. No wonder we turned out like we did. We didn't get no help from him. Said he wouldn't give us anything unless we went to college and cleaned up our acts. College. What a waste of time."

"No. He didn't really do that to you?"

"Yeah, he sure did. It's all a mess." She sat back and belched and wiped her mouth with the back of her hand. "It just didn't turn out right. Now, we ain't sure what to do."

"Tell me more about it. I'd like to help if I can." He leaned in toward her as much as he dared.

She looked at him and smiled before a blank look

covered her face. She leaned over her plate with both hands flat on either side of her on the booth seat. She burped again. "I gotta go to the bathroom. I don't feel so good."

Stratton moved away from her quickly as she heaved herself out of the booth and practically ran to the restroom.

His pinkie ring slightly tapped his beer bottle as he reached for it. He sipped his beer. Thoughts ran around in his head. *I should be tailing Emma, not sitting here,* was the most prominent in his mind.

He tapped the bottle. He drank more beer. As he checked his watch, he caught movement out the window.

Willow's van squealed out of the parking lot.

He sighed and motioned for the waitress to bring the check. "She must not have cared for my company after all," he said to himself.

"Miss H. Do you remember how to spell my name?"

"Sure I do. Why?" Emma said into her phone.

"Just checking. I have data on Mr. Klinn."

"Great. I'm on my way there now. Hold on." She pulled her truck over in an empty landscaping company parking lot, got her notebook and pen out of her purse, wrote "BARTENDER" on the top of a clean page, hit the speaker phone button on her cell, and laid it on the dash.

"Okay, what do you have for me?"

"Mr. Laniford Klinn, spelled L-A-N-I-F-O-R-D.—K-L-I-N-N is twenty-six years old and has many, many money troubles."

"How many?"

"He is in foreclosure on his house, three months delinquent on his loan payments on a bar called The Blue Caboose, and he is five months behind on his used car lot rent, Klinn's Kleen Kars." Merek spelled out the company name. "He is in debt up to his *dupa*."

That's one Polish word Emma recognized. It meant ass.

"Right. Interesting. Only twenty-six. Same age as Alder and Tammy. He sure looks older," she jotted notes.

"He went to the town high school and middle school, no college. Divorced last year, one daughter, four years old. Seems to be current on child support payments, but everything else he is behind."

She jotted notes in her notebook. "Anything else?"

"Yes. One more thing."

Silence.

"Well, are you going to tell me?"

"This is a dooz-oh, as you say in America."

"A dooz-*ee*. Anyway, what is it?"

"Mr. Klinn has a restraining order against him."

"Filed by?"

There were a few more seconds of silence before Merek said, "Tammy Mycon."

"Tammy Mycon? Oh! Wait. Tammy Eastland?"

"Bingo, Miss H. You are one sharp cookie."

"Tammy Eastland?"

"We just said this, did we not?"

"Tammy Eastland. How long ago?"

"Four years."

"Well, well, well, now. Isn't that something?"

"A horse of a different painting, you might say."

"It's a sharp knife and a horse of a different color. Anyway...okay. Let me think."

"I am not the one who stops you from doing that, Miss H."

"Funny. Hey, you know, Merek..."

"Yes, Miss H?"

"You know—"

"You could not live without me?"

"That's right."

"I have to scram. Big date tonight."

"Seems like everyone's got a Thursday night date. Which tall blonde are you taking to the Wildflower for dinner tonight?" Emma asked.

Merek laughed. "You tell Detective Joey he should not tell about my business. Polish men are known to be very private people. I can make him sorry."

"Right. You can run over him with your Harley sometime."

Silence.

"Merek?"

"Miss H. I must ask, if I stopped working for you, what *would* you do?"

Emma laughed. "You're kidding, right?"

"We will talk when you get back. I gotta scram."

The call clicked off and she put her cell back in her purse. Shaking her head she dropped the Tacoma into drive and headed toward The Blue Caboose.

"What is up with him?" she said aloud.

Lanny Klinn was behind the bar again and Jebediah sat in the same booth where Emma had met him six nights prior. She walked up to the bar and smiled at Lanny.

"Hi, Lanny. How's it going?"

He gave her a dirty look. "You like this place so much you came back, huh?"

"Actually, no. I think it's a dump and if I were with the health department, I'd shut you down. But I'm meeting Jeb over there for dinner. He says this place has the best burgers in town. Hope there's no cockroaches in them."

Lanny's cheeks turned red above his beard. "I'll see what I can arrange."

"You do that. Hey, do you know who owns this joint? When I was in here the other night, the ladies room needed a serious cleaning. Enough to call the health department about, I mean." She glared at him.

He stared back and tossed the bar rag toward her, barely missing her. She didn't flinch. "I'll get someone on it."

"That'd be great."

She sauntered over to Jeb as best she could do in her six-inch heels and short tight skirt. He didn't bother standing or removing his hands from around his beer bottle. He looked up at her, gave her a once over and his mouth fell open.

"Hey, good looking. What do I have to do to get a drink around here?"

"You should've asked Lanny," he finally said.

"Who's Lanny?"

"The bartender."

"Oh, you know him?" Emma asked, sliding into the booth opposite Jeb.

"Been coming here for years. Know his whole family. His dad helped me out when I locked my keys in my car few nights back. You could say I do."

Emma watched him for a few seconds, looked over toward the bar and back at Jeb. "What else do you know about Lanny? My cousin thinks he's cute."

"Who's your cousin again?"

"Charlene."

"Right."

"She was only in here a couple of times and saw the bartender there, Lanny, and thought he was cute. Is he single?"

Jeb gave her a long look. "Why you so interested in Lanny?"

"*I'm* not. Like I said, it's for Charlene. This is what girls do for other girls. Investigate. You know. Find out stuff about guys for each other. Anyway, you probably know lots of people around town, don't you?"

"I guess." He looked away. Emma didn't want to lose him by asking too many questions.

"So, how do we get service around here?" she leaned over and touched his arm.

"You have to go tell Lanny. Don't think he's got much help tonight. Only saw one new girl waiting tables in the back."

She looked at him. *What a romantic.*

"Any menus in this place?"

Jeb pointed to a chalk board hanging above the booth between them. Emma leaned over so that her cleavage was front and center in Jeb's face. She lingered over the table as she read the smudged writing.

She sat back down, patted her helmet hairdo, and smoothed her top, pulling it down a little lower. Jeb smiled and took a sip of his Bud.

"Well, you said the burgers were good, so I'll have a burger, a bag of chips, and a Bud." She looked at him, glanced toward the bar and back at Jeb.

He stared at her for a few seconds before he finally pulled himself out of the booth and walked to the bar.

# CHAPTER 15

It was going on nine-fifteen when Jeb wiped his mouth on a greasy paper napkin and tossed it on his Styrofoam plate. Lanny strolled over, gave Emma a disgusted look, and cleared the table.

Emma smiled at him. "Would you please bring him another beer and I'll have a glass of water," she said.

"Sure thing, *missy*." Lanny snarled at her.

"What's *his* problem?" Emma asked Jeb after Lanny walked away.

"He's got lots of problems."

"Yeah. Like what?"

"I don't know. Just got lots of problems, like the rest of us, I guess."

Emma looked toward the bar. Lanny was a small man who reminded her of an unhappy troll.

"So, tell me more about your hunting. You a good shot?"

"I am. I'm one of the best," he said, sitting up straighter.

"You ever shoot anything?"

"Well, sure. Deer. Squirrel. Rabbits. Went elk hunting once with my brother, couldn't get a bead on one though."

"You ever shoot a person?"

"That's a dumb question. I don't hunt people." He leaned back and looked at her like she was an idiot.

"Ever think about it?"

"What kind of question is that?"

She shrugged. "I was just talking, is all. I read in the paper about that woman that got arrested for shooting her ex-husband on Paint Creek this past weekend. You hear about that?"

"Yeah. I heard."

"And?"

"And, what?"

"Do you think she did it?"

"Sure. They arrested her so I guess she did."

"Do you know Tammy Eastland?"

"I know of her, alright. She's Taylor Eastland's too-young-of-a-wife, is who she is."

"Why do you say that?"

He shrugged. "He's old enough to be her grandpa, that's all."

"Really?"

"Almost."

"So, what's wrong with that?"

Jeb shrugged. "She had men chasin' after her all her life and she ends up with *him*." He shook his head and took a long drink.

"Taylor Eastland. Hey, where have I seen that name around?" Emma snapped her fingers beside her head.

"He's a realtor. He sold my mom her house. Sells houses to everybody all over the county. Well, he used to sell the houses, now Tammy does. She sells the houses and he sells business stuff."

"Oh, right. *That's* where I saw the name. On 'For Sale' signs."

"Taylor Eastland's the most honest man as you can come by around these parts. He doesn't even cheat at poker."

Emma felt her ears start to ring.

"You don't say. You two friends? Doesn't sound like you like his wife much."

Jeb shrugged. "I don't like her. But I like Taylor alright. Everyone around town likes him."

The door opened and Emma and Jeb both looked

up. Stratton walked in, looked around, barely gave Emma a glance and walked toward the back of the bar. He *really* was the most handsome man she'd ever seen in her life. Her stomach did that little flip. She quickly turned back to Jeb.

"So how long have you played poker?"

"I don't play much, just every now and then."

"Where do you play?"

"At some friends', sometimes at Taylor's."

"When's the last time you played at Taylors?"

He shrugged. "Probably a couple weeks ago or so. My buddy Joe said they were short, so I went. Didn't play too good that night either. I lost a lot of money—about ten bucks." He took a swig of his beer.

Emma's face got hot.

Lanny approached their table with a cocky stride.

"Do you know that guy that got shot? Alder Mycon?" Emma asked Jeb as Lanny stopped at their table with their drinks. He stood tall before he set another Bud in front of Jeb and slammed her glass of water in front of her so hard some of it splashed out onto her top. He tossed the bill on the table, turned, and walked into the back room as Emma wiped off her top with a napkin.

She glanced over Jeb's shoulder. Stratton smiled at the waitress and ordered. Out of nowhere, two women sidled up beside him and started flirting. He nodded and motioned for them to sit down with him. Emma's stomach rolled and she felt she'd burst into flames. She turned her eyes back to Jeb and frowned.

"That was a shitty thing to do. What kind of bartender is he?" She continued to wipe her top before she tossed the wet tissue on the table and glanced toward Stratton again. She suddenly felt she had to get away from Jeb and every man.

"You know, I don't feel well. I feel like I might be

getting the flu or something. I think I'd better go back to my cousin's and rest. I'm sorry. I was hoping we could go to a movie."

Jeb narrowed his eyes, stared at her, and took another long swig of beer. "Well, ain't that a shame? You in town often?"

"No. Not too much. But the next time I am, I'll call you. I promise."

"So, you're ready to go home? Now?"

She nodded and squished up her face like she'd eaten a lemon. "Yeah, I'm sorry. But we had a nice dinner and got to know each other better." She reached over and patted his arm.

"I guess." He finished his beer and set it hard on the table.

She stood, nearly toppling over. She was used to wearing water sandals and flats, not spiked heels. She pulled down her skirt and hiked up her tube top.

He stood and looked her over several times.

"I guess you still want me to pay for dinner?" he asked, disgusted, picking up the bill.

"No, not at all. Let's split it."

"Yeah, that'd be good. It's pretty steep; about twelve bucks."

"All the more reason to help out," she said, smiling. She pulled out a twenty and put it in his hand. "Give the rest to the bartender as a tip. He deserves it for his great service."

Jeb looked confused by her sarcasm as they walked toward the bar together. He paid the waitress at the cash register while Emma waited by the door, glancing at Stratton again. He was laughing. So were the girls.

Jeb walked Emma to her truck. She opened the driver's side door, standing partially behind it, purposely putting it between them.

"Well, thanks again. I had a good time. I hope you

did, too. I'm sorry I don't feel well."

The door to the bar opened and Stratton walked out and toward his Silverado, parked on the other side of the lot.

Jeb shrugged, clearly unhappy. Emma knew she'd ruined his plans for her and the evening, but she really didn't care. They would've been ruined no matter what she did or didn't do.

"Yeah. I guess." He turned and walked toward his Saturn.

"Hey, I'll call you again the next time I'm in town. I promise."

He shrugged, frowned, got into his car and slammed the door.

She climbed into her truck, not an easy task in her outfit and shoes, and pulled out of the parking lot. She was fuming mad. "So this is his game, huh? Well, I should've played it too. I'm just too damn mad. I can't believe that man!"

After driving for several blocks, she glanced in her rearview mirror. Headlights followed her and she smiled. Now, she wanted to crawl into the king-size bed with Stratton and fall asleep in his arms. "What emotional roller coasters relationships can be," she said to herself.

Twenty minutes later Emma pulled into the B&B's parking lot, turned off her truck, and started for the door. Half-way there, a small car squealed into the lot, nearly hitting her.

"Hey! What the—" she yelled. Her heart thumped in her chest as she stood inches from the bumper of a brown Saturn. Jeb jumped from the driver's side and ran toward her. She turned and tried to sprint for the door, nearly turning an ankle. He caught her arm.

"You come here right now. Who are you? I saw you at the lake with that man that came in the bar. I want to know who you are. Asking all those questions and looking like you did. Who are you anyway?"

She turned, faced him, and regained her balance. He came toward her. She grabbed his arm with her other hand and jerked him hard toward her. It pulled him off balance and he sailed past her. His face slid on the asphalt when he hit the ground. He got up on his hands and knees while she flipped off her stilettoes and threw her purse in the flowerbed.

She round-house kicked him hard in the ribs before he could stand. He went down with a huff.

As he groaned and tried to get to his feet, she chopped him across the back of the neck and he sprawled on the ground again.

"I suggest you be careful who you're grabbing, Mr. Pierce," she said.

Jeb rolled onto his back as Stratton's truck squealed into the drive behind them. He jumped out and ran to Emma who had just found her purse in the bed of mums and black-eyed Susans.

Stratton grabbed her and held her in his arms. "Emma, honey. Are you alright? I was following him, but he lost me." He kissed the top of her head and held her.

"I'm in better shape than he is. I'll call Day," she mumbled into his chest, pulling away, and brushing off her purse. She got her cell out of her purse and called the sheriff's office.

Jeb rolled onto his back, moaning. Stratton walked over and looked down at him. "You move and I'll make sure you *never* get up."

# CHAPTER 16

Charles was in his king-sized bed, staring at the ceiling. He'd finally put the food away, put his pajamas on, and gone to bed around one in the morning. He'd paced the house for hours while calling and sending texts to the number on the text message he'd received from Simon yesterday. There was no reply. Nothing. He scoured the Internet, Facebook, and LinkedIn several times, as he often did. Nothing.

The alarm beeped at six. He hit the off button, got up, and stepped over the boys. They woke up and followed him down the hallway. He opened the sliding back door and they filed out. He shut it, turned, leaned against the granite countertop, and dropped his head in his hands. He rubbed his face, looked up, and screamed toward the ceiling, "I am NOT going to let you destroy me again, Simon Johnson. I will NOT."

He busied himself grinding coffee and putting it in the coffee machine. He poured dog food and water in each of the three sets of dog bowls. He put away the dog food, got his favorite mug from the cupboard and placed it on the counter before he let the boys back in the kitchen. They scurried to their bowls and sounds of crunching, munching, moaning, snorting, tags clinking on the ceramic bowls, toenails-tapping, a tail thumping the wall and water slurping filled the air; the standard morning sounds.

He went back to his bedroom, showered, and dressed for work. As he stood in front of the full-length mirror, his cell rang as it lay under the Tiffany lamp on the nightstand. He ran to it, picked it up, and sighed.

"Good morning, Janet."

"You don't sound like you're having one. Something wrong?"

He said nothing.

"You okay?" she asked.

"Peachy."

"Peachy? In all the years I've known you, you've never once said you were 'peachy.'"

He sighed. "Please get to the point."

"Alright. My sister's visiting with her kids today and they want to go to the park. I was going to take Murray and the boys, but wanted to clear it with you first. Is that okay?"

"Whatever you want to do. I don't care." He nearly shouted into the phone.

"Charles, why are you so angry? Did I do something wrong?"

"No, Janet. I'm sorry. I'm terribly sorry. I just got up and I didn't sleep the entire night. Not a single wink. I do apologize." He took a deep breath.

"I understand. I've had those kind of nights. Hey, after I pick up the dogs in a bit, you could get some shut-eye. Give you some quiet time in the house."

"No. I don't need to be alone in this house right now. In fact, I need to talk to you about how far you'd travel to take care of the boys."

"What?"

"I'm calling a realtor this morning. I'm putting the house on the market."

"Charles, what's going on? Just yesterday you told me how much you loved that house. It was the perfect neighborhood and you had the best yard for the boys and the best dog sitter and neighbor in the world–me."

"I'm aware of my statement then, but circumstances have changed. Not the part concerning you, of course, but there are other dynamics I can't discuss."

186

"Since when? Why?"

"Since I've decided to move. It's time. I need something different, something that's not, I don't know, not as big. Maybe a condo. No yard work."

"A condo? Charles, your landscaper makes sure you have one of the most beautiful yards in Clintonville and where are the boys supposed to play? That's one of the things you told me you liked about that house is that huge, vinyl-fenced back yard of yours. You just had it re-landscaped this summer. What's going on? Tell me."

He said nothing.

"Well, I'll be over in about fifteen minutes to get the boys if you'd like to talk about it. You have coffee on?"

"Yes," he said.

"Good. Can you save me cup and we'll talk for a few minutes?"

"Certainly."

"Okay. Bye."

Charles hit the icon on his phone to end the call. He stared at it for several seconds before he hurled it onto the tile floor.

Emma and Stratton sat across from each other at the dining room table eating their Friday morning breakfast of eggs, bacon, sausage, muffins, freshly ground coffee, and a choice of tomato or freshly-squeezed orange juice. The clock on the mantel chimed ten-thirty. Stratton was devouring his food while Emma picked at her eggs. Lucky waddled in.

"Hey, girl. How you doing?" Emma asked.

Lucky glanced at Emma, wagged her tail, walked over to a bed in the corner, and flopped down with a wheezy grunt. Robert and Clara had gone on a pet-supply shopping extravaganza and now Lucky had a plush doggie bed in nearly every room of the house. They were acting like brooding grandparents-to-be.

"Lucky looks miserable," Emma said to Robert as he walked in with another tray of muffins and set them on the table.

"She's just eaten her breakfast and the vet said those puppies are sure to arrive any minute," he said.

He glanced at Stratton. "Talking to the sheriff last evening must've made you hungry, Mr. Reeves."

"It did. And, you're a wonderful cook, Robert," he answered between bites.

"Why thank you. I'm so glad you enjoy it."

"Speaking of Lucky, we're lucky Stratton made it home the way those two women had him sandwiched between them at the Blue Caboose last night," Emma said, picking at her eggs.

"You should eat, Emma. After what you went-through last night. I still can't believe you didn't file charges against that mongrel," Stratton said, ignoring Emma's comment. Robert picked up a few dishes and left the room.

She shrugged. "I can't believe he didn't file them against *me*. Jebediah is just a lonely guy who lives with his mother and likes to hunt and fish. He seemed a lot nicer after we actually told him who we were. Poor little thing. He was my main suspect in this thing, until Day questioned him and checked out his alibi.

"Jeb was at work Saturday morning during the shooting. I did see money in his shirt pocket. He told Day he'd stopped by a bank on his way to the bar and cashed his check at a grocery store, shoved the cash into a white envelope, and had it in his pocket when I came over and sat down with him. Checked out. The clerk remembered him. It couldn't have been Jeb that shot

Alder.

"And he did just happen to be fishing at Ross Lake while we were paddling, although I'm not sure I completely buy that coincidence. He still swears he doesn't know Forrest Mycon, and never talked to him, but the bartender, Lanny, told me they were talking before I went in there. That's stuck in the back of my head."

Emma picked up her coffee and shook her head. She stared at Stratton over the rim. She put the cup back in the china saucer.

"You want to know what's really been bugging me?"

Stratton chewed his bacon and raised his eyebrows, giving her a *"No, I don't, but I'm sure you'll tell me"* look.

"How did Forrest know who I saw running through the woods? He was too far away and he was involved in helping Alder. And I know Day didn't tell them what I reported to her and I haven't told anyone but you and Charles.

"And why are he and Willow so hell-bent that it's Tammy? She has no motive as far as I'm concerned. She has a new life, a new baby on the way. Why would she want to shoot Alder? And why does she have a restraining order against Lanny, the bartender?"

She gazed out the window for a moment and continued. "And how would she know Alder would be on that creek? Everything is pointing right at her, especially that rifle and Day told me Tammy was seen by several people pumping gas into her muddy Jeep at the gas station right before the shooting. Why would she be that stupid?"

"Maybe she didn't have enough gas to get to the put-in." he said.

"Right. Oh, golly gee, I'm planning to shoot my ex-husband, but I forget to gas up? I'm not buying it. I think you're still high from that thick perfume last night."

Stratton wiped his mouth and laid the napkin on the table. "Alright. I see your point, dear. But, now, listen. I need to talk to you about something very serious."

She stared at him. "What is it?"

He sat back and sighed. "When I was on the phone with Rhonda yesterday, Chief Lawrence came in while we were talking, so she hung up. Lawrence called me back and told me he wanted to talk to me about Earl Calhoon."

Emma looked confused. "Calhoon? He's in jail until his trial, whenever that will be. Why would Lawrence want to talk to you about him? Did he have more information for your story?"

Stratton held her look for a few seconds. "Because he's *not* in jail. He's escaped and Lawrence is afraid he may be on his way up here, looking for you."

Emma's shoulders dropped and she looked away. She sat there for several seconds. "Shit," she whispered.

"I didn't mention it to you until now because, well, frankly, this whole Willow and Jeb ordeal took up the entire day and evening and we've both been absorbed with it, and you're not in Clintonville, so I wasn't overly worried that he'd find you here. I decided to wait to tell you. But, Emma, darling, we both know, if someone wants to find someone these days, it's not at all difficult. We need to think about this, seriously. He's a dangerous man and he's on the loose. You didn't mention your being here on your Facebook page, did you?"

She shook her head. "No."

"Good."

The clock ticked on the mantel. Lucky snored softly. Robert and Clara laughed together in the kitchen. Emma's cell buzzed on the table. She looked at the number and grabbed it.

"Hey, Joey. You got that DNA back yet?" She

smiled broadly. "You don't say. Well, well. Thanks, Joey. I owe you."

Emma listened for a few seconds before she laughed.

"Alright. I'll look at it on the B&B computer, no problem. Oh, and be careful. Merek informed me he doesn't like you telling me about his personal business. He may run over you with his Harley."

She listened. She frowned.

"What? No, he hasn't said anything to me about it but that explains why he's been acting so funny on the phone. No, I'll let him tell me when he's ready. No, that's okay. Don't worry about it.

"Hey, when I get back, dinner on me, your choice." Silence.

She leaned back in her chair. "No problem. Don't worry about it. I'm not going to tell him you told me or that I know. Thanks, Joey."

She hit the end button on her cell and frowned at Stratton.

"You're not going to tell who that you know what?"

"It's Merek. Joey told me Merek's tall blonde-of-the-day told him they were moving to Denver. Must be what he needs to talk to me about. Damn it!" She smacked the table.

"Merek is moving?"

"Sounds that way."

"Oh, honey, I'm sorry. He'll be hard to replace."

"No doubt."

She stared at the table, threw her napkin on her plate, and dropped her face in her hands. Stratton reached across the table and rubbed her arm. She looked up and took his hand.

"I need to call Tammy," she said.

"Okay."

She picked up her phone and checked the recently

called numbers, then hit the send key. Taylor Eastland answered on the third ring.

"Good morning, Mr. Eastland. This is Emma Haines."

"Good morning, Ms. Haines. I'm not at all finished with your list, but we're working on it."

"Good, I'll want it as soon as you can get it to me. Could I speak to Tammy, please?"

"I'll put her on." A few seconds of silence passed before Tammy came on the line.

"Yes?"

"Hi, Tammy. How are you doing?"

"Okay I guess. I can't sleep and I can't take anything either. I'm so tired. Did you find out anything."

"Well, yes, as a matter of fact, I did. Tammy, you need to be totally honest with me here."

"About what?"

"Why you filed a restraining order against Lanny Klinn four years ago?"

The phone went silent. "Let me call you right back." She hung up.

Emma set her cell on the table and frowned at it, her arms crossed in front of her.

"What'd she say?" Stratton asked.

"She'd call me right back."

"Think she will?"

"She'd better."

They sat in silence. Emma watched Lucky. Stratton watched Emma.

About a minute later her cell buzzed. It was a number that she couldn't recall, but it was the local area code.

"I hope this is her," Emma said, lifting the cell to her ear.

"Hello?"

"It's me. How did you find that out?"

"Tammy, it's not hard. I'm a former insurance fraud investigator. I train investigators. It's public information and court records. And there's this thing called the Internet."

The phone was silent for a few seconds.

"Lanny wanted to marry me. We dated a few times in high school, but I started dating Alder and married him. But Lanny wouldn't leave me alone. Look, Taylor doesn't know about any of this."

"Does Alder?"

Silence, then a soft, "Yes."

"So Alder knows Lanny wouldn't leave you alone and you had to file a restraining order against him?"

"Yes."

"So I'm guessing Lanny doesn't like your ex-husband too much and probably not Taylor, either."

"Look, I just wanted Lanny to leave me alone and be done with it. I haven't heard from him or seen him since, so to me, it's over. Talyor needn't know about any of this, so I'd appreciate you keeping this to yourself. I don't need any more trouble."

Emma sighed. *Has this woman been chased by every man in town,* she thought as she watched Stratton shovel a piece of pancake into his mouth. Then, *how does he stay in such great shape for his age and eat like a horse?*

"You're right about that. You don't need any more trouble. Okay. Unless I have a reason to tell him, but —"

"You don't, so don't do it. Look I have to go lie down. I'm totally exhausted and I don't feel like talking about this anymore and I can't upset the baby. Taylor will be looking for me too. He thinks I'm in the bathroom. I had to come out to the office to call you back. Listen, Miss Haines, if you can't help me, then we'll hire someone who can. If all you're going to do is dig up dirt about me, well, I just don't know if I want to talk to you anymore."

"Tammy, you can hire whomever you want. But I am trying to help you. And Alder too."

"Well, I hope so. Good-bye."

The call went dead.

Emma rolled her eyes and slid her cell in her purse, which was hanging on the back of her chair. She gazed out the window for several seconds before she got up and went into the small study at the B&B. She opened her email and scanned the list of kayaks registered in Ross County and logged out.

She returned to the dining room and gave Stratton a hug around the neck from behind. She nibbled on his ear lobe.

"Wipe your mouth, dear. We're going to go look at cars," she said to Stratton.

"Cars?"

"Yes. Cars."

Emma pulled into the lot of Klinn's Kleen Kars and drove slowly up and down the four aisles of vehicles ranging from those that looked like they were on their way to the crusher to a few shiny brand new models.

Clouds were building and the sky was growing dark.

"What are we looking for?" Stratton asked, scanning the lot.

"I'll know it when I see it. Like I told you, Joey said the hair's not real. It's from a wig and it had traces of plastic on it, like from a plastic bag or trash bag. And something Jeb said to me while we were on our date hit me while I was talking to Merek so I followed my gut. Now, I want to know more about Laniford Klinn."

"What did Jeb say?"

"He said Lanny's dad had helped him out when he'd locked his keys in his car. I can't believe I didn't think anything about it at the time, but it just slipped by me.

"While you were in bed snoring your little head off this morning, my sweet, I looked up locksmiths in the phone book that Robert keeps in the kitchen on the shelf by the phone. I found a family-owned and operated Klinn's Keys, and he has a locksmith shop here in town. The ad said it's been in town for forty years. I'd bet money that's Lanny's daddy and Lanny worked with him at some point."

"So Lanny Klinn would know how to pick a lock," he said.

Emma nodded. "Exactly. Then Merek called and told me about a restraining order Tammy filed against Lanny. They'd dated in high school, so Lanny would probably know that Tammy's a sharpshooter and he'd probably know that Tammy had that rifle. And Tammy just confirmed to me that Lanny feels no love for Alder or Taylor or Tammy."

"I see where you're heading with this," he said as she drove around the back of what appeared to be the sales office; a small brown metal building with a rusted door that was padlocked.

Behind the metal building, she slammed on the brakes. "And Lanny Klinn has access to lots of cars. I kept reading my notes and then it all just clicked in my head this morning. Bingo!" she said as she pointed.

A red Jeep Liberty, exactly like Tammy Eastland's, sat in tall weeds behind the paved lot. Emma nearly jumped out of her truck before she threw it into park. She ran to the Jeep, squatted down in front of it and examined it. Stratton got out of the truck and followed.

"He didn't get all the mud off. Look."

He stooped beside her.

Every crack and crevasse on the car was caked with

dirt and mud. She made her way around the Jeep. Two kayaks – one red and one green – were partially hidden in the brush behind the Jeep.

"This is the Jeep that Charles and I saw at the put-in and those are the boats that Forrest borrowed from *his friend*. They're both registered to Laniford Klinn."

"I can't believe he didn't get rid of all this," Stratton said.

"He needs money and it's a nice car and boats. He's probably planning on selling them. Desperate people often do stupid things," she said.

Stratton nodded. "That's for sure. Just read any newspaper."

She examined the surroundings. A small dumpster sat about forty feet away beside the parking lot.

"Hey, big guy," she winked at Stratton. "Want to go check out that dumpster for me?"

"Some date you are," he said, smiling and shaking his head. He turned and walked over to the dumpster and opened the lid. Emma followed.

"Give me a lift up," she said.

"Don't make me mad or I'll throw you in."

He braided his fingers and she put her right foot in his hands and steadied herself against the side of the dumpster and his shoulders. He slowly lifted her. She leaned over the top of the dumpster and peered in. A green trash bag lay on the top of a stack of cardboard boxes. She stretched, but couldn't reach it.

"Can you push me up just a little higher?"

He raised her a few more inches.

"Uummmpppph, ohhhh, aahhh, noooooooo" she yelled as she toppled over into the dumpster.

"Emma! Emma! Are you alright?" Stratton tried to pull himself up to see inside the dumpster.

She had landed softly on the stack of cardboard boxes. She lay there and looked up at the sky. She started laughing uncontrollably. "I'm fine. Just remind me not to ask you for a lift into another dumpster real soon," she yelled between laughs.

She got herself together, stood on the boxes, and balanced herself before she grabbed the green garbage bag and tossed it over the edge. It plopped to the ground beside the dumpster.

"I'm coming out now, think you can help me?" she yelled. She jumped up on the side of the dumpster and swung a leg over. Stratton helped her down.

"You okay, my little dumpster diver?" he asked through a chuckle.

"I'm fine. Your idea of a boost was a little more than I needed. Glad there was just cardboard boxes and that bag in there," she said.

"Sorry about that."

She brushed herself off. "You'll pay for it."

"Oh, no. Not another date with Willow, I hope."

She walked toward the bag. She leaned down and untied it. Inside were a blue jacket and a wig of long black hair. "Yes!" she shouted, with exuberance.

Stratton started to say something, but was interrupted by the sound of a roaring engine. A large green SUV came tearing into the lot. Seconds later, Lanny stood in front of them with a gun. He fired a shot and a loud clank sounded off the dumpster.

Stratton fell to the ground.

Emma dropped to her knees and leaned over him. He was face down on the ground, blood spreading through the gravel from under his right side.

"Oh, my, God. Stratton! Stratton!" She looked up and saw Lanny walking slowly toward her with a handgun in his right hand, aiming it at her.

"We need to get him to a hospital," she screamed. "Help me!"

Lanny walked closer, lowering the gun to his side.

"Who's he?"

"He's my boyfriend."

"Shit. Is he dead? Oh, hell. I didn't mean to hit nobody. I just meant to scare you off. I aimed at the dumpster. You're on my property. You're trespassing." He bent a little closer to Stratton. "Oh, shit, no."

Emma looked down at Stratton. Hot tears ran down her cheeks. She clenched her jaws so tightly she thought her teeth would break. She felt his neck. His pulse was strong.

She looked up at Lanny and stood slowly, her fists balled at her sides. Her heart pounded in her ears. She walked slowly toward him, robotically raising one foot at a time, as though she was in a trance.

He stared at her, took two steps back, and dropped the gun.

She darted toward him and threw a kick to his stomach. He grunted, bent, turned, and ran toward his truck. She ran to her truck to get her phone.

Lanny was about five feet from his truck when a rusted blue pickup came squealing into the lot and stopped. Forrest jumped out of the driver's side with a gun in his hand, aiming it at Lanny.

"Lanny Klinn, I told you Saturday night that we ain't giving you no more money. You didn't do the job you promised you would. You missed," he yelled.

Emma grabbed her purse, squatted toward the ground, turned, and made her way back to Stratton. She bent in front of him. He rolled over, trying to get up on his knees.

"Stratton, don't move. You've been shot, but you're okay. Stay down."

He nodded. "I don't think it's bad. I don't have any pain." He held his side.

POW! The sound ricocheted through the trees.

"Take cover," she yelled.

She helped him scuttle behind the dumpster into the tall weeds. She turned and crawled back to the dumpster on her belly and peeked around the side.

"I still can't believe you missed. Some damn shot you are," Forrest yelled at Lanny.

"I must've knocked the scope on a tree when I was walking through the woods," Lanny yelled back.

"Don't matter why. We ain't givin' you no more money. We can't get it since you didn't kill him. We won't get the farm now. You messed up everything. We hired you to kill him and you missed. And you said you were the best. I should've had Willow do it, but she ain't no shot and she's too fat to run through the woods or wear a coat like Tammy's. But she'd probably a' done a better job than you."

"I did most of the job and I need more money. I got the gun and put it back and Tammy's going to jail. You can kill your brother yourself, you damn chicken shit," Lanny yelled.

Forrest raised his gun and fired. The back windshield of Lanny's SUV exploded. Lanny froze.

The sound of sirens filled the air. Forrest lowered the gun and looked behind him as he started to get in his truck.

It began to rain.

Sheriff Day and four other cruisers pulled in, blocking him the drive, throwing gravel and dirt. Armed deputies jumped out of the cruisers, aiming rifles at the two men.

"Drop your weapons and put your hands in the air!" Day yelled through a bullhorn.

They did as they were told.

# CHAPTER 17

Charles shook the realtor's hand and closed the front door behind her. He watched out the bay window as she pounded the "For Sale" sign into the ground, then went to her sedan, and pulled away.

He went into the kitchen, gathered his keys and wallet and left for the office.

WOSU 89.7 was on the radio playing the classical music that Charles found soothing. His stomach growled and he checked his watch. It was only eleven; too early for lunch and too late for breakfast.

As Henry Purcell's *Minuet in A Minor* came through his Bose speakers, he ran through his thoughts. He was as done with Simon Johnson as he'd ever been. Being stood up by him last evening was the absolute final straw. He was either going to be crushed by the pain all over again or this time he was going to really try to get over it once and for all. When the iPhone had shattered on his kitchen tile floor, it was like something finally exploded inside him that said, "Enough."

He and Simon had met at an engineering conference and had immediately been attracted to one another. Simon was from a wealthy oil family in Texas. He wanted nothing to do with the family business and found a teaching job at The Ohio State University. After they'd been together a few years, his trust account kicked in. This gave Simon the freedom to be the house-husband for several years until he decided to start a small consulting business. It was more for the fun involved than the money, plus it got him out of the house. Simon didn't need to worry about money. His trust account could take care of him for his lifetime and then some.

Charles never understood how they'd fallen so in love and spent nearly a quarter-of-a-century together only to have it all come to this. But it had. Wishing that it hadn't happened wouldn't make the ending any different. He couldn't change the past. He'd also never understood why Simon moved to Spain, of all places, since he'd never mentioned it to anyone or even visited the country. At least, not that Charles knew about. He simply walked out on Charles and his consulting firm without a word. No one knew why.

As he'd watched the pieces of his iPhone slide across the floor, he'd made the sudden decision to sell the house and move; maybe even look into a transfer out of the country. He'd been approached many times, but had always said no, hoping in the back of his mind that Simon would come back – to their house.

*And what about Ron? Will he ever talk to me again?* Charles couldn't blame him if he wouldn't.

He reached for his iPhone out of habit and remembered it was in his kitchen trash. He'd have to make a trip to Verizon sometime today.

He pulled into the parking spot with his name and position displayed on the sign in gold lettering and put his SUV into gear. He stared at the sign for several seconds: Charles Wellington, Chief Engineer. He lifted his head high, and took a deep breath.

"To hell with you, Simon Johnson," he said, gripping the steering wheel.

He got out of his SUV, grabbed his briefcase from the back passenger seat, locked the vehicle, and headed to his office.

"Good morning, Kathy. Would you please call the Verizon store on High Street and have them get another iPhone ready for me to pick up? I dropped mine and it's no longer functional. Any messages?" he asked as he stood in front of her desk.

Kathy stood slowly. "There's someone here to see you. He's in the public building."

"Who is it?"

She paused. Charles gave her a puzzled look. There was no color in her face.

"Kathy, what's wrong?" His stomach knotted. *Simon.*

"It's a man who says he's your father. He's been waiting for more than two hours."

Charles stared at her.

"Hold all my calls and get security on the phone. Tell them to meet me there."

"Yes, sir."

He walked back to the hallway door, zipped his security pass card through it, and turned right toward the elevators.

He walked through the underground walkway to the public building and into the waiting area. His father jumped from the chair and turned to face him, holding his worn wool hat in his hands. He wore the same polyester suit and brown scuffed shoes he'd worn at Mary's.

They stared at one another for a long moment.

"Exactly what are you doing here?" Charles finally asked.

"Any problems here, Mr. Wellington?" a security guard, the size of bus, asked from behind him.

Charles said nothing, not moving his eyes from the older man standing in front of him.

"I came to apologize and tell you I won't bother you

anymore. It seemed important to come and see you one more time before I go. I just want to talk to you," the old man said.

"I thought you left on a flight for home, compliments of mother."

"I changed my ticket at the layover in Vegas and came back. I just want to talk to you. Please?"

Charles looked at the security guard. "We'll talk in the public conference room, over there. Could you please see we're not disturbed?"

"Yes, sir."

They walked into a small conference room and Charles motioned for the man to sit down as the door closed behind them. The security guard stood outside.

"Please, sit down," Charles said as he took the seat at the head of the oak conference table.

His father slowly sat down across from him. He looked small and meek in the black leather chair. He put his hat on the table in front of him.

Charles took a deep breath then looked into his father's tired gray eyes.

"Mr. Wellington, I do not know you at all. By all the information I have, you're down on your luck. You left your wife and baby fifty-seven years ago, and now you show up here looking for a handout. Your behavior is preposterous. I cannot believe you're here. You have no right. This is unacceptable."

Wellington, Sr. shifted his weight.

"I am not looking for a handout. I don't want or expect anything from either of you." He stiffened. "I don't mean any harm. I just wanted to talk to you." He leaned on the table with his chest. "I just want to tell you something, and then I'll go away and never bother you or your mother again. I swear."

Charles glared at the man, his left pinky twitching uncontrollably. He covered it with his right hand. "Say what you have to say and then security must escort you off the premises."

"Your mother is not telling you the truth. I did not run away after you were born. Your mother and I never got along. But when she told me she was pregnant, I knew I had to marry her and help raise you. I had to do the right thing." He stopped.

They looked at each other.

"Go on," Charles said.

His father nodded. "She's the one who kicked me out. I didn't want to go, but I did, and decided to move as far away from her as I could get and start a new life. I told her she could stay on the family estate as long as she wanted. I never liked the place, myself. I'm not a farmer and neither were my parents. I wanted to sell it, move to the city and get a good job to support you both. But neither Mary nor my parents, who lived in California at the time, would agree with me.

"My father always wanted to live in California, so they moved, thinking I would take over the estate in Circleville. So, yes, I did leave. But it was Mary's doing, not mine. I stayed with my parents for a while before I got a job and my own place. I was a janitor for a business in Silicon Valley for years. Good job, good pay. I loved working around all the technology and the work kept me in shape. Then I got laid off and my wife was diagnosed with cancer. She died in February. The hospital was so good to her, I decided to volunteer there. That's what I do now. I've had a hard time finding another job at my age.

"My parents – your grandparents – they were crazy about your mother, but they didn't know her. Behind her sweet front, she's a stubborn, evil woman. I'm sorry to say that about your mother, but she is. Every year that I was gone, I tried to contact her to ask if I could come to see you. She never answered my letters or my phone calls. I sent her support checks every month, but they were always returned unopened. I finally gave up."

Charles stared at his father. "I'm very sorry about the loss of your wife."

"Thank you."

The room fell silent.

"Did you ever ask her about me?" Charles's father asked.

"No. She mentioned your leaving once when I was quite young. We never discussed it again."

The man gave Charles a long look. "Did she? And did she tell you the *real* truth? Or was it *her* truth?"

Charles flashed back through his mind and realized that he and Mary had never really discussed his father's departure. She said that the topic wasn't up for discussion—ever—and that they were both better off without him. They lived their lives in luxury from Mary's golfing and Charles really never gave it any thought.

The old man spoke up again. "I'm not a wealthy man, but I have my pride. Soon after I moved to California, I met a woman, a truly wonderful woman, and I wanted to marry her. But your mother refused to give me a divorce, even though she wanted nothing to do with me. I was like a toy to her, someone she could bat around. But finally, the divorce came through. We married and lived happily together. But as I mentioned, she passed away about seven months ago. I never understood your mother, but it doesn't really matter anymore."

"Is this what you needed to tell me?"

The man nodded. "That's all. I truly regret not being able to be a part of your life, but you've grown into a fine young man. Mary did a fine job. I'm proud of you, Charles. That's all I wanted to tell you." The man smiled broadly.

Charles couldn't help but return the smile. "Thank you. Yes, mother did a fine job raising me. Mr. Wellington, I—"

The intercom on the table buzzed.

Charles looked at it, annoyed, noticed Kathy's name and number, and picked up the receiver.

"Kathy, I'm—"

"Charles, it's Emma. It's an emergency. She's on line two."

"I'll take it in my office. I'll be right up." He replaced the receiver on the phone, stood, and looked at his father.

Wellington, Sr. stood and walked around the table to Charles and put his hand toward him.

Charles shook his father's hand.

"Thank you for listening to me — and have a wonderful life. I just needed to see you. That's all. Now I have to get a cab to the airport."

"I'll have my secretary call one for you."

"Thank you, Charles. I'd appreciate that. Goodbye. Oh, and, I have that, too, and so did your grandfather."

Charles looked at him quizzically. "Have what, too?"

Wellington, Sr., raised his left hand. His pinky was twitching. He smiled at Charles, turned and walked past the security guard.

Charles and the security guard followed slowly. His father walked through the lobby, out the front door of Bridge Systems, put on his hat, and sat on a bench.

Charles watched him for several seconds before he pulled out his cash clip and peeled off eleven fifty dollar bills. He handed them to the security guard.

"Please give this to him and make sure he doesn't attempt to return it."

The security guard looked at the cash and glanced out the window at the old, frail man sitting on the bench. He turned back to Charles and smiled slightly. "Yes, sir."

"Thank you."

Charles turned and walked hurriedly down the hall. He hit the button on the elevator, cursing himself for having smashed his phone. Emma had probably been trying to call him.

When he finally got to the sixth floor, he ran down the hallway, past Kathy, into his office and shut the door behind him. He went quickly to his desk, hit line two, and picked up the phone.

"Emma? What's wrong?"

"Oh, Charles," she sniffled. "I'm at the hospital. Stratton's been shot."

"What?"

"I cracked the case all right and nearly got him killed." Her voice trembled.

"What's his condition?"

"He was hit on his right side. The bullet went through the flesh. A scrape, really. He was so lucky."

"Well, that's good, I'll be down there in an hour."

"Okay. Thank you." She sniffled again. "He's in room 402. And, Charles?"

"Yes?"

"Get here quick. I need you."

"I'm leaving now."

He hung up the phone. Seconds later, Kathy tapped on his door and let herself in.

"Charles, what can I do to help?"

"I have to go back to Chillicothe. Emma's boyfriend's been shot."

"Oh, no. That's horrible."

"He's probably in better shape than she is, from the sound of her. I've never known her to be this upset."

"Well, I'm sorry."

Charles gave her a look. "I know you two don't get

along, so, thank you. Could you please call Janet and explain the situation. I'll call her later myself—when I get another phone."

"Certainly. Be careful."

"Thank you."

Charles walked into room 402. Emma ran to him and hugged him—hard. He hugged her back. It felt good.

Stratton looked like he had just gotten back from the barber. He was glowing, propped up on pillows in the bed. He waved to Charles.

"Hey, Charles. Emma said you were coming. It really wasn't necessary."

"Of course, it was. Don't be ridiculous," he said as he and Emma walked over to the side of his bed. "How are you?"

Stratton raised his arms and let them drop on the bed. "Bored. They're letting me out of here as soon as the doctor comes. Bullet went right through me, pretty much a little hole in my side; just a few little stitches. It's really not a big deal. Good thing I put a few pounds on this week." He laughed.

"It *is* a big deal. You were shot," she said.

"Just a nick," he smiled at her as the doctor walked in, flipping through Stratton's chart.

"You'll have to wait outside. I need to examine Mr. Reeves and sign his release if everything looks good," the doctor said, barely looking up from the clipboard.

Emma bent over and kissed Stratton on the cheek.

He patted her arm. "Go get the truck warmed up, honey. Let's go home," he said.

"Emma, I've never seen you so distraught," Charles

said to her as they stood outside Stratton's door in the hallway.

She gave him a look. "Where's your cell? I tried calling you for over an hour," she said, ignoring his comment.

"It became inoperable. I'll have to replace it."

"I can't imagine how you felt about *that*."

"You have no idea."

"I'll bet. Anyway, let's go sit down over there and talk." She motioned to a small waiting area about twenty feet from them.

They sat down.

Charles crossed his legs at the ankle, made a steeple with his hands, and rested his index fingers on his lip as he waited for her to go on.

"I was so scared when I saw Stratton hit the ground. I've never been that scared and pissed off at the same time in my entire life."

"Except perhaps in West Virginia." he said.

She looked at him. "Well, yeah. When I thought you'd been shot by Calhoon. Oh, and I have to tell you about that, too." She sighed and looked at the floor. She went on to explain what had transpired over the past week. Charles, as always, listened without interrupting, a trait Emma admired in him.

"So, it was Lanny, the bartender at the Blue Caboose, not Jeb or Tammy or Taylor. At least she'll be cleared. My gut told me it wasn't her after I met her," she said.

"It's amazing that you remembered what Jeb had mentioned about locking his keys in his car and how you connected it to his father's locksmith shop. Phenomenal job, Emma. You're quite keen at connecting the dots in these matters. I applaud you. However, let's get to the heart of the matter."

"What do you mean?"

"Don't play ignorant with me. Something's happened which you had little control over."

"What are you talking about?"

"You've fallen in love with Stratton and it's eating you alive."

"It is not."

"So you admit you're in love with him."

She opened her mouth to speak, but shut it and looked at him. She nodded slowly. "And it scares the hell out of me. It's going to change my whole life and then it'll cause nothing but pain in the end." She regretted the last comment as soon as it passed her lips. She glanced away. A long silence fell between them.

"Does Stratton make you happy?"

"Well, yeah. I mean, I enjoy being with him and I miss him when he's not around. I actually called him and asked him to come up here. He drove up here through the middle of the night and snuck into my room at the B&B – and then he ends up getting shot."

He looked at her for a long time before he said, "Emma, that's not your fault, so stop blaming yourself."

She sighed. "I know. Nothing is anyone's fault anymore, right? Just life unfolding." She gestured, palms facing the ceiling. A tear ran down her cheek and she brushed it off quickly.

Charles put his hand on her arm. "He's fine. He's being released. It was only stitches. That's all. It's not your fault. It's not his fault."

"But he could've been killed."

"Emma, you and Stratton could've been killed when you laid that trap for Pearl in West Virginia. But things hadn't progressed so far between the two of you; you barely knew him. Now, this. Perhaps you should consider letting the authorities handle these situations in the future. Have you learned anything at all from these incidents?"

She pursed her lips and frowned at him.

"I mean it. You need to stop chasing criminals and simply kayak and train the investigators at the insurance companies to catch the villains. And now, you say Calhoon's on the loose. I mean, that could be catastrophic. You need to stop this nonsense."

"But, it's what I do," she said.

"It's what you *did*. Isn't that why you quit being a fraud investigator and started H.I.T.? So you wouldn't have to chase hoodlums and be shot at any longer?"

"I don't want to talk about this anymore." She flopped back in her chair and crossed her arms in front of her chest. They sat in silence for several minutes.

"On top of everything else, I think Merek's leaving me, moving to Denver."

"Now, *that* would be catastrophic. You may have to actually work and cut down on your kayaking."

"Very funny."

"Why's he moving to Denver?"

"A blonde."

"I see. Well, it was bound to happen at some point. He's young and really has nothing other than his job keeping him here. But I am sorry. He will be difficult to replace."

"I know."

They sat, looking at the carpeting. Emma started tapping her Skechers on the floor. She took a deep breath, sat tall and looked at Charles.

"So, how have *you* been?" she asked.

He didn't answer for several seconds. "I've had several challenges myself."

"What kind?"

"I seem to have—"

"Excuse me," the doctor said, standing to the side of the waiting area.

Emma and Charles stood.

"Mr. Reeves is free to leave. He's waiting for you."

"So he's fine?"

"He is. He just needs to keep the wound clean and no heavy lifting for two weeks. Other than that, no restrictions."

"Thank you," she said before she ran into Stratton's room.

Charles smiled, sadly.

# CHAPTER 18

At eleven thirty on Friday evening, Charles sat on the front porch of the First Capital B&B wearing his silk pajamas and a heavy throw wrapped around him. He leaned back in the white wicker chair. Emma, Stratton, the Shaws, and six other guests had gone to bed several hours ago, but he couldn't sleep. He stared down the empty street.

The temperature was in the low forties, warm for a mid-October evening in southern Ohio. Everything was quiet except for the leaves that swirled and chased each other down the street, as if running playfully from a breeze. The wind chime on the porch tinkled and he pulled the throw tighter around himself and leaned back.

He'd heard nothing from Simon and even if he had, Charles had decided it was over and he never wanted to hear from his former partner again. He was finished with leaving any options open for him to ever return, which from all appearances, wasn't going to happen anyway. He figured Simon must've definitely had second thoughts and was probably already back in Spain, getting on with his life. Charles decided he needed to finally – really – do the same.

"How could you do this to me?" he whispered aloud. He thought of Mary and his father claiming that Mary had kicked him out. He couldn't get his father off his mind.

Everyone would be going back home to Clintonville in the morning. Stratton would stay at Emma's before they flew to Europe. Charles would return to his work and his life and re-write his resume and make a few calls about jobs overseas. He hoped his house would sell soon. He wished he could talk with Ron, but he doubted that would happen, either.

He felt his whole life – everything – had totally changed in the past week. His friends, even Simon, left the country to refresh themselves with different countries and cultures. Maybe he should do the same.

Emma had Stratton now and he knew their time together would begin to infringe on his and Emma's time together. While he was happy for them, the thought of Emma no longer being in his life as she'd been for the past sixteen years made him sad. And now Merek was leaving too. He sank lower in the chair and sat staring down the street, thinking.

The front door creaked open and Charles shot up in his chair, but relaxed as Emma peeked around the screen door. "What are you doing out here?" she whispered.

He smiled and gestured for her to join him.

She opened the door, closed it behind her, and sat beside him in the matching wicker chair. She pulled her robe up higher around her neck and tightened it around her waist. Her basset hound slippers stared up at her.

"Where on earth did you find those slippers?" he asked.

She smiled at them as she lifted them off the floor several times, making the ears bounce. "The Ohio Basset Rescue. I bought them at the basset fest last fall."

"They're *certainly*...stylish." He smiled.

"Thanks. Murray was jealous of them at first, but he got used to them."

"How is the master basset?"

"He's fine. Spoiled and stubborn, as always. I can't wait to see him tomorrow. He and Maggie get along great, thank goodness. How're the boys?"

Charles took a deep breath. "They're fine. Just fine. I'm looking forward to being with them, too."

A cricket began chirping. "Wow, he's hanging around late. I haven't heard a cricket in weeks," she said. They sat in silence for several minutes. "Charles, tell me what's been going on in your life. I miss you." She reached over and took his hand. He squeezed it.

"I miss you too." They sat holding hands as he told her about the satellite, his father, Simon, and Ron.

"Why didn't you tell me about all this?" she asked.

Charles turned his head and gazed at her. "I didn't see the need to burden you. You've been busy."

"That is the dumbest—"

"Is it? Emma, our relationship has changed, as all relationships do. You've been spending a great deal of time with Stratton and you'll be spending much more time with him, from what I can see. And, I'm truly happy for you."

He gazed down the street. "Everything changes constantly in this life. Lately, I've found it particularly unsettling. But, it's time for me to change too. I've put my house on the market."

Emma stared at him.

"Your house? For sale? What? Moving? What are you talking about? Where are you going?"

He turned and looked at her. "I'm not sure."

A car passed. Leaves rustled in the trees. The light from the streetlamps winked through the swaying branches. The porch swing swung hauntingly. They sat in silence for several minutes.

"When Stratton and I come back from Europe, you and I should take a trip, a long one. Take the boats and the dogs and talk this through. No chasing bad guys, either. I promise." She gave him a sad smile, kissed him on the cheek, and squeezed his hand.

"I'd like that."

Saturday morning Emma, Stratton, and Sheriff Day sat at the Eastland's table drinking coffee. Charles had received a call from his realtor that she had three showings scheduled for his house and he'd already left for Clintonville.

"I appreciate your help, again, Miss Haines, but you realize you broke the law by withholding evidence, not to mention your other smooth moves. If you weren't such a good investigator and friends of several respected law enforcers, I'd take you in."

"I know. I know. And I'm really sorry about all that. But I wanted to make sure the hair didn't belong to a long-haired squirrel before I called you. Thought I'd save you some hassle, get it done a little quicker." She smiled at Day.

The corners of Day's mouth raised slightly.

"Well, we can't thank you enough," Taylor said, squeezing Tammy's hand.

"That's right. I still can't believe you were shot, Mr. Reeves. I'm so sorry," Tammy said.

"Another shooter with bad aim. Saved me in Vietnam too," he said.

Emma gave him a sad smile as she remembered seeing the scar on his chest for the first time. He'd told her the story behind it and she'd cried softly as he stroked her hair.

He winked at her. Her stomach did that little flip. *My God, he is so gorgeous,* she thought.

"That's another thing. You shouldn't have gone to the car lot at all," Day said, giving Emma a dissatisfied look as she took a sip of her coffee. "You should've called me and told me what you suspected."

"How did you know to come to the car lot?" Emma

asked. "Did someone report gunfire?"

Day shook her head. "Willow called and tipped us off. She said that Lanny had been demanding more money, for a job he, thankfully, didn't succeed in completing. She said her brother had just left her place, raging mad, and that he had a gun. He knew that Lanny was at the car lot and he told Willow he was going to make sure Lanny didn't ask them for any more money. She also said that some man *from the FBI* took her to dinner and asked her all types of questions about her brothers. She was afraid she and Forrest were going to prison and thought it might help if she confessed – like they do on TV."

Day glanced at Stratton. He smiled, raised his eyebrows, and looked away.

"When we pulled in, I was more than surprised to see you two there."

Everyone sat in silence for a few moments.

Emma said, "Well, I felt early on that Forrest and Willow were behind Alder's shooting, but I didn't know how. They both knew what I saw in the woods, they were both broke and desperate for money. By killing Alder and getting the farm, which they wouldn't have anyway because of the way the will was written, they thought they could inherit it, sell it, pay Lanny off, and split the rest. They hired him because they knew he hunted a lot, could pick a lock, and he disliked Tammy about as much as they did. It was a scheme they cooked up months ago, probably when they were all drunk or high."

Emma turned to Taylor and Tammy, "Lanny broke into your house and took your gun. He fired it at Alder and then replaced it while you were both out of the house."

She looked at Tammy. "Remember when you told me that last Saturday you sat in a house waiting for a woman to come for you to show it to her and she never showed?"

Tammy nodded. "Yes, the house on Haydensham Road. I waited for over an hour. The woman sounded very excited about buying."

"She would because it was Willow who called you, disguising her voice, to get you out of your office, alone, away from your office manager. While you were sitting in that house, you were also seen pumping gas at the gas station and driving to the put-in below Bainbridge.

"The three of them thought they had it all figured out. Kill Alder, get the money, and put you in prison by making a big show out of framing you. A crazy scheme, but I've seen worse."

"But what about the Jeep being covered in mud. It hasn't rained here for the past several weeks." Taylor asked.

"I had Merek check into when Lanny got that Jeep. It was during a series of rain showers in the area a few months ago. Easy enough to find a big mud puddle and smear the Jeep and hide it until they needed it. This was certainly a premeditated frame-up job."

She took a sip of her coffee before she continued. "Anyway, I really thought for a while that it was Jeb. After all, he's a hunter, and there was that white envelope that looked like it had money in it. Which it did. He'd just cashed his paycheck. I thought Forrest gave it to him for the shooting before I walked into the bar that night. Lanny told me that Forrest had talked to Jeb. Obviously, Lanny lied to throw me off him. And, coincidentally, Jeb had been here playing poker a few weeks ago.

"But it turns out, Jeb really doesn't know Forrest Mycon. I guess we all make mistakes."

# CHAPTER 19

It seemed like years instead of only seven months since they'd left the Mycon family situation back in Chillicothe. Even after spending five weeks in Europe together, Stratton still hadn't popped the question. From the vibes Emma was sending, he feared it might damage their relationship and he was content with the way it was going. At her invitation, he'd moved into her Clintonville condo, using the guest room as an office. He'd promoted Rhonda to manager, and hired two reporters to run the *Stonefalls Post* back in West Virginia, while he remained the chief editor.

Stratton and Emma had been working long hours and decided to take a weekend kayak trip on the Red River in east-central Kentucky.

Stratton drove his Silverado slowly through the Nada Tunnel in the Red River Gorge located in the Daniel Boone State Forest. Emma rode in the passenger seat and their kayaks were in the bed of the truck.

"Isn't this cool?" Emma asked.

"Pretty cool."

"A tunnel, right through the mountain. This was built by a lumber company around 1910 so they could get the timber out of the area. A train used to run through here. I drove through a mountain tunnel in Alaska when I was going to the kayak livery at Prince William Sound. It took about a half hour to get through it and you had to ride on the railroad tracks. The cars and trains took turns going through it," she said.

"I've been through that tunnel. I believe it's the

Whittier Tunnel."

"That's it. Anyway, I didn't get to kayak. The wind never died down. I was pretty bummed about it."

"Well, we'll have to go there and try again."

"Okay," she said. "I'm game. It'll have to be awhile though. Calvin Nelson keeps lining up project after project for me. I mean, I'm not complaining, I like the work, but it just seems nuts. He's a strange one. He's always looking at me and telling me he loves me."

"Do I need to have a talk with Mr. Nelson?"

"No, daddy. I can take care of myself."

"Well, let me know if I do. I can understand why he's in love with you, but you're taken."

She gave him a look with a crooked smile.

"I'm just glad Merek took my offer to be a full partner and let that blonde chick ride west into the sunset without him."

"Yes. From what you told me about the scene she'd made in your office when Merek refused to go with her, sounds like it was best for everyone involved.

"Oh, yes. You should've seen the fit she threw. Merek thanked me a dozen times after she went roaring off on her Harley for keeping him from making a *wspaniały błąd*–great mistake." She sat back in the seat and sighed. "Ahhhh, right now, life is good."

"That it is. It'll be even better when they catch Calhoon," Stratton said.

Emma said nothing. A Johnny Cash CD Stratton had been playing was beginning on the third song.

"Is that CD almost over?" she asked.

"Not quite. Why? Would you like to hear more?"

She crossed her arms in front of her chest and gave him a dirty look.

He chuckled. "Now, I have to listen to a lot of YES and that Jon Anderson fellow, that band called The Fixx, and Led Zeppelin whenever you drive. Honestly, it gives me a headache, but it's your truck."

"Well, this music makes me want to throw myself under your tires and beg you to run over me," she said, looking out the window. "You like the classical and jazz I play sometimes."

He reached over and shut off the CD player.

She turned to him. "You didn't have to shut it off. It's your truck. Your music."

"Oh, no. I wouldn't want you to jump out and become a speed bump on my account," he said.

"Why do you listen to that stuff anyway? It's so depressing."

"Not at all. It's real. It's feeling. It makes sense. You can understand him. He sings about love and loss. He sings about life."

"I'm glad there's different kinds of music." She turned to the side window. They rode in silence for a few minutes until she said, "Look at those wildflowers blooming already."

"They're beautiful. Do you think we'll need to wear our jackets on the river? Hard to believe it's supposed to be in eighties today and it's only the middle of April. We certainly lucked out on the weather this weekend," he said.

"Well, we are five hours south from Clintonville, but it's always cooler on the water and we'll be in the gorge. I'd take it with you just in case."

He nodded.

She turned in her seat to look up at the valley walls. "This place is so beautiful and not that far of a drive. We should come down here more often."

"Yes, it is. I can't wait to get on the water so I can look at it instead of this road," he said.

She turned back in her seat and looked at Stratton. "Do you think Charles will move to Switzerland?"

"I don't know. He certainly has a great offer."

"Yeah. I nearly fell off my chair when he told me."

"It really bothers you, that you're not with him very much anymore, doesn't it?" Stratton asked, not taking his eyes of the curving highway.

"I still can't believe he sold his house the week he put it on the market and moved into a rental. I mean, the new house is nice and all, and at least it's still in Clintonville, but his house was so perfect. And now he's never home. He's either traveling for work or staying in California with his dad. I just miss him. We were tight for a lot of years."

"I know. But you and I both know he knows what he's doing," Stratton said.

"Yeah. I do. He's trying to move on and keep busy. No Simon. No Ron. *No me.* And he's really been spending a lot of time with his dad. Mary would disown him if she ever found out."

"I think he's a wonderful person; an intelligent, kind and caring man. Maybe Switzerland is what he needs," Stratton said.

"Maybe. All I know is that he and I need to take a long weekend trip again, especially if he takes that job. I haven't really talked to him much since we sat on the porch at the B&B that last night in Chillicothe."

He patted her leg. "Well, we can always go visit him, you know. I've not been to Switzerland."

"I know. But it's just not the same between us anymore. We've really grown apart. It's just sad."

"I know, honey. But it's life."

"Like Johnny Cash sings about?"

"Exactly." He smiled at her. "Life changes, Emma. People come and go, in and out, all the time. Nothing lasts forever."

"I know. But it doesn't make it any easier."

"No, it doesn't. Not to change the subject, but did you remember to tell Janet to give Maggie her aspirin with her dinner?"

"Yes, I did. I'm glad she and Murray get along. I think he really digs that golden gal." She laughed.

"Me too."

"Don't forget. We're keeping the boys next week while Charles is gone and Janet's on vacation."

"Right. Everyone chips in where our four-legged children are concerned," he said.

She sighed toward the window, turned and leaned over the truck console and gave Stratton a peck on the cheek.

"What was that for?" he asked.

She shrugged. "My lips were cold."

"Ahhhh, glad I could help out."

He pulled down into the boat launch turn-around off Rt. 715 and parked in the sandy lot under the stone bridge beside the Red River. They unloaded their kayaks and gear. Emma's truck was at the take-out, about twelve miles downstream.

Stratton moved his truck to the parking lot at the top of the hill and walked back down the road to the turnaround.

They grabbed their belongings, tossed them in their kayaks, and carried them to the water's edge. Emma walked between the bows carrying them by the handles. Stratton held onto the carry handles on the sterns. They slowly descended the stone stairs down to the water, set the bows of their boats in the water, put on their life jackets, got into their kayaks, and started paddling down the Red River.

"That was a nice hike to the top of the Natural Bridge last evening. It was perfect timing," Stratton said.

"Sure was. I haven't watched a sunset like that in years."

"And Miguel's is a fun place too. I enjoyed the pizza."

"Good," she said. "I knew you'd like it. It's fun to see all the rock climbers that go in there. They travel from all over the world to scale these walls."

They continued downstream, talking about the beautiful scenery in the gorge and their plans for the evening while a man stood on the stone bridge watching them through a pair of binoculars.

**TO BE CONTINUED**

# About the Author

Trudy Brandenburg is an avid kayaker and writer. Over the past thirteen years, she has paddled on many rivers and lakes, the North Atlantic and North Pacific oceans, and the Gulf of Mexico. She is a member of the Southern Ohio Floaters Association (SOFA) paddling club, based in her hometown of Chillicothe, Ohio.

Her published works have appeared in *Quirk's Marketing Research Review; The Consultant*, published by the Association of Consulting Foresters; various online publications; poetry books; *Holistic Discoveries* magazine, and in various newsletters. She also published a CD, *Whitelight Relaxation Meditation*. She's been a researcher and writer at an insurance company for the past twenty-two years. This is her second novel.

When she's not kayaking or writing or reading or riding her bicycle or playing her piano or creating her designer greeting cards, she's strolling through her Clintonville, Ohio, neighborhood with her basset hound, Millie.

For future release dates and appearances, check out Trudy on Facebook or at www.trudybrandenburg.com.

She may be contacted for signings and speaking engagements at trudy@trudybrandenburg.com.

Made in the USA
Charleston, SC
16 July 2014